C4 656320 00 E1

D1179419

Accidentally educated in the sciences, **Kelly Hunter** has always had a weakness for fairytales, fantasy worlds, and losing herself in a good book. Husband...yes. Children...two boys. Cooking and cleaning...sigh. Sports... no, not really—in spite of the best efforts of her family. Gardening...yes. Roses, of course. Kelly was born in Australia and has travelled extensively. Although she enjoys living and working in different parts of the world, she still calls Australia home.

Kelly's novels SLEEPING PARTNER and REVEALED: A PRINCE AND A PREGNANCY were both finalists for the Romance Writers of America RITA® Award, in the Best Contemporary Series Romance category!

Visit Kelly online at www.kellyhunter.net

FLIRTING WITH INTENT

BY
KELLY HUNTER

MILLS & BOON

First published in Great Britain 2011
by Mills & Boon, an imprint of Harlequin (UK) Limited,
Eton House, 18-24 Paradise Road, Richmond, Surrey TW9 1SR

© Kelly Hunter 2011

ISBN: 978 0 263 22099 5

Harlequin (UK) policy is to use papers that are natural, renewable and recyclable products and made from wood grown in sustainable forests. The logging and manufacturing process conform to the legal environmental regulations of the country of origin.

Printed and bound in Great Britain
by CPI Antony Rowe, Chippenham, Wiltshire

Also by Kelly Hunter:

THE MAN SHE LOVES TO HATE
WITH THIS FLING…
RED-HOT RENEGADE
UNTAMEABLE ROGUE
REVEALED: A PRINCE AND A PREGNANCY
EXPOSED: MISBEHAVING WITH THE MAGNATE
PLAYBOY BOSS, LIVE-IN MISTRESS
THE MAVERICK'S GREEK ISLAND MISTRESS
SLEEPING PARTNER

**Did you know these are also available as eBooks?
Visit www.millsandboon.co.uk**

CHAPTER ONE

CHRISTMAS was commerce and retail excess. Christmas was family and sometimes it was farce.

Add to the day a wide-open wallet and a city bathed in neon and the memory of a Hong Kong Christmas burned brightly for ever. Ruby Maguire—born to riches and living in Hong Kong for over six years now—knew this from experience. Which meant that she should have been able to organise a perfectly splendid Christmas for the children of one of Hong Kong's foremost investment bankers in her sleep.

A trip to Hong Kong Disney or Ocean Park. A holographic Christmas tree or three. More presents than they knew what to do with, a mad mix of Christmas lanterns and fake winter wonderlands and, if Santa was *really* on the ball, maybe their charming, handsome, super-important father would put in an appearance and make their day.

Except that the West children were all grown up these days, and, from the snippets of information Russell West's executive PA had let slip, Russell's eldest son was unlikely to be in attendance, his firstborn daughter was recovering from serious injury, his other daughter was a reclusive genius, and his fourth-born—

another son—was either a crime lord, a charming wastrel or James Bond.

So much for taking them to Disneyland.

Instead, Ruby had decked the halls of Russell West's pristine marble penthouse with as much high-class folly as she could find. White orchids; real ones. Poinsettias; silk ones. Tapered white candles just waiting to be lit and more fat goldfish for the glass-covered pond. The pond ran beneath the base of the stairs and along the atrium wall until it reached the tiny rooftop terrace where the songbirds reigned supreme. The only thing missing from the scene was a pet cricket in a bamboo cage. For Australian-born Russell West, owning a pet cricket was taking cultural assimilation one chirrup too far.

December twenty-second already, with the three younger West siblings due to arrive tomorrow. Upon arrival they would find immaculately prepared rooms, festive touches in the strangest places, and reservations for one of Hong Kong's premier restaurants, should they wish to dine out.

Ruby wasn't a housekeeper or a cook, though her current job strayed into such territory at times. She far preferred to think of herself as Russell West's social accountant—a position created just for her, out of pity most likely, but she'd tried to make herself useful, and the hefty bonus Russell had just presented her with gave credence to the notion that he thought her service of value.

She wrote Russell's charity dinner speeches, briefed him on the changes in status of Hong Kong's elite, and basically made his social engagements as stress-free and fruitful as possible.

Ruby's latest challenge had been the buying of Christmas gifts for the children of Russell's employees—an endeavour she had seen to with pleasure. Furthermore, Russell now had an up-to-date database citing the names, birthdates and interests of his employees' spouses and children. She'd even done one for the wives and children of his major business contacts. Whether Russell would *use* the information remained to be seen.

Trust a financial wizard to pay absolutely no attention whatsoever to the little things that went such a long way towards the cultivation of solid business relationships in Hong Kong.

As for the choosing of gifts for his *own* children; be they genius, wounded, idle, or missing…that was Ruby's job too and she had approximately twenty-four hours to do it in. Russell hadn't even given her a price range, let alone a guide as to what type of gifts they might enjoy.

'Not even a hint,' she muttered to herself as she dumped the box of sparkling mineral water on the kitchen counter and opened the French doors leading out to the terrace. 'It's not right.' She plucked a pair of thin plastic gloves from the terrace cupboard and headed for the songbird enclosure.

No tiny bamboo cages for these little oriental white-eyes but a large bamboo aviary that ran the length of the courtyard wall and incorporated branches and greenery, nesting and feeding areas, and a newspaper lined roll-out litter tray that Ruby refreshed every day. Western, very Western, and a source of no little amusement to many of Russell's acquaintances, but the birds sang their pleasure, and both Ruby and her employer took pride in the freedom of movement the little birds enjoyed.

'There should be a rule that says a father should damn well buy Christmas gifts for his children *himself*,' she told the flitty little birds who clung to the side of the cage in greeting. 'Why is that such a stretch?'

'Beats me,' said an amused male voice from the direction of the kitchen, and Ruby glanced around, eyes widening at the splendid vision that had just presented for her perusal. A raven-haired blue-eyed stranger stood just inside the terrace doors, wearing nothing but a snowy-white towel that rode low on his hips and clung lovingly to well-packed thighs. His chest was bare, his shoulders impressive. *Not* an everyday sight in penthouse sixty-one.

'Who are you?' she said as she straightened from her crouching position, the roll of bird-dropping stained newspaper still firmly in hand.

'My thoughts exactly,' he murmured with a grin that put Ruby in mind of mischief and at least one other thing she really shouldn't be thinking about if this was indeed one of Russell's sons.

'I'm Russell West's social organiser,' she said, ignoring that lazy smile as best she could. 'And you must be one of his sons. Trouble is, which one?' She let her gaze drift once more over his very fine form. 'One of you I wasn't expecting until tomorrow. The other one I wasn't expecting at all.'

'I could be the pool boy.'

'Yes, and I have absolutely no doubt that you'd make an excellent one, but alas there is no pool.' Ruby continued to study him. 'You'd think I'd be able to tell the difference between a mission-fatigued special intelligence officer and a feckless rogue by now, but you know what?' Ruby shook her head. 'You could be either.'

'I've never had an insult wrapped so skilfully inside a compliment before,' he murmured, that devilish gaze of his not leaving her face. 'You must practise.'

'And you must be Damon,' she guessed. 'Russell's youngest.'

Ruby dumped the soiled newspaper into the mulching bin, peeled off her gloves and brought forth her manners and her hand. 'I'm Ruby Maguire. I'm looking after Christmas for your father.'

'I see.' Damon West had a nice touch. Firm but not bone-crunching. A man fully aware of his own strength. 'How's that working out for you?'

'So-so,' she said and took back her hand. 'Your sisters are due in on flights tomorrow afternoon. I'm afraid there's no word from your brother.'

Ruby watched a shadow steal across Damon West's well-cut face. She was an only child with a raft of step-siblings she tended to avoid. Family politics was not her forte and she had no intention of getting involved in the West family's woes. 'I gather you've made yourself at home?' There were half a dozen bedrooms in the marble delight, each with en-suite. 'You've been here before, right? You don't need the grand tour?'

'Right.'

'Coffee?' Ruby headed for the wondrous stainless-steel-and-glass kitchen and set to washing her hands in the sink there. 'Tea? Cold drink? I'm hoping it's too early for gin but you never know in the tropics.'

'It's too early for gin,' Damon said and padded over to the other side of the counter. 'Coffee would be good. Espresso if it's an option.'

'It's an option.'

'So…Ruby. You live here?' he asked just a little too casually as she set up the coffee machine and took a cup from the cupboard.

'Hardly. No one lives here, unless you count your father sleeping here on occasion and entertaining here every so often. I feed the fish and the birds, water the plants, pick up your father's dry-cleaning, stock the fridge, organise housekeeping and gardening and pre-pare for house guests.'

'Has this always been your lot in life?'

'No. In another life I was a law graduate working my way through the corporate law system but that all fell through when my father the investment banker de-cided to go to the Caymans rather than to prison. It was a good call on his part. The prisons here aren't very nice.' Ruby opened the fridge and reached for the sugar bowl. 'Sweetener?'

'You're Harry Maguire's daughter?'

'Guilty.' She set the sugar down in front of him and leaned forward, elbows on the counter, wondering just what it was about this man that made her want to poke at him. 'I'd never have taken you for someone who reads the finance pages?'

'Sweetheart, your daddy skimming eight hundred and seventy-two million dollars in point-one-cent in-crements and then disappearing into the ether didn't

only make the finance pages. He's quite the crime star.'
Damon crooked his head in what Ruby decided was reluctant admiration. 'So, where is he now?'

'That's the eight-hundred-and-seventy-two-million-
dollar question, Damon. And truthfully, I have no idea.'

'You weren't close?'

'We were very close.' Ruby dropped her gaze to the
glossy countertop and gave him the truth. 'I grew up in
a family of two. Me and my father and a never-ending
raft of nannies, butlers, cooks and tutors. I worshipped
the ground he walked on. Now I don't.'

'Because he broke the law? Or because he left you
behind?' asked Damon West gently and Ruby looked at
him, really looked at him, and she didn't see a charming
wastrel any more. She saw a man who knew his way
around the dark places of a person's psyche. One who
seemed entirely comfortable dealing in shades of grey.

'The law's a slippery thing, Damon.'

'So it is.' Damon leaned across the counter as if to
meet her halfway.

Hard not to let her gaze linger on his mouth but she
managed. Hard not to enjoy the potent mix of lazy intensity in his eyes and wonder whether or not it would
carry through into the bedroom. A betting woman
would have to go with yes.

'Do you have any plans for the day?' she asked, for
it was definitely time to change the subject.

'What are you suggesting?'

'Oh, I don't know. You. Me.' She had his absolute
attention. 'Christmas gift shopping for your sisters.'

He drew back abruptly and Ruby smiled, wide and
warm. 'Gotcha,' she whispered, rocking forward ever

so slightly before turning back to the coffee maker to
retrieve his espresso and set the machine up for a long
black for herself. 'Do you really think I can afford to
proposition the adored son of the only man in Hong
Kong who'll employ me? Trust me, I'm not that reckless.'

'I'm not that adored.'

'Yes, you are, Damon. You'd only have to listen to
the way your father talks about you to realise that. He
speaks of you with a mixture of love, frustration, pride
and respect, and I have to confess: the first couple are
what I'd expect of most fathers, but that last one...the
fact that one of the most influential money movers in
the world respects *you*... Makes me wonder what you've
done to earn it.'

'Keep wondering,' he murmured. 'I'm all in favour of
keeping a fine mind exercised. As for going Christmas
shopping with you, the answer is a reluctant yes. Give
me five minutes to put some clothes on.'

'Good idea. Take your time. I'll need about fifteen
to finish up here anyway.' Ruby pushed the tiny cup of
super-strong coffee across the counter towards him and
Damon West's fingers brushed hers as he took it. This
time his touch sent desire skittering along her skin, and
Ruby frowned as she whipped her fingers away from
his. What the *hell* was that?

Apart from a rhetorical question for she knew desire when she felt it, knew the bite of it and the chaos it
could bring. The question now became how could she
have let this happen? Between one touch of hands and
the next?

To *her* of all people. Ruby Maguire, who'd been out-playing players her entire life.

'What's wrong?' Lazy smile on a dangerous man. 'Coffee too hot?'

'That's one interpretation.' Ruby sighed. 'Regretfully, I'm going to have to ban the touching from now on in. And the teasing. Probably the question time as well. Sorry, Damon. I can't afford to play with you.'

'Because you work for my father? Would he really have to know?'

'Damon, please. I'm insulted that you even *tried* that line on me. Your father may not keep up with the so-cial lives of all his business acquaintances—that's my job—but when it comes to the romantic liaisons of his children? Men like your father?' Ruby slanted him a quelling glance as she topped up her long black with cold water before lifting it to her lips. 'They always know.'

Ruby Maguire was a babe, decided Damon as he took his coffee back to his bedroom. A high-maintenance glossily gift-wrapped bundle of temptation and contra-diction, and what was more she knew it.

Damon couldn't have asked for a better distraction.

Something to take his mind off a missing brother and a wounded sister and a Christmas that was shaping up to be anything but festive.

He slung his towel on the bed and rummaged through the meagre collection of clothes he kept at his father's house. A collared cotton shirt in white and a charcoal pinstriped suit. Bespoke, not made to measure. The expensive sports watch that his sisters had given him

last Christmas. Clothes to suit his father's house and reflect his father's status—a Christmas tradition whereby
Damon would look to be the type of son his father expected to see and in return his father would ask no questions as to what Damon had been up to the rest of the
year.

What kind of man had Ruby Maguire's father been
before his fall from grace? wondered Damon as he
tossed the suit on the bed. Already a wealthy one, if
he remembered correctly. Manhattan banking family.
Influential. Chances were that Harry Maguire hadn't
stolen the money because he'd needed it.

Maybe he'd been bored.

And colour Damon perceptive but the delectable
Ruby Maguire also seemed somewhat overqualified
for her current gofer position.

Ruby Maguire was used to dealing with the corporate lions of the world and holding her own. Ruby had
severely underestimated her usefulness if she thought
that no one but his father would employ her.

Which made Damon feel infinitely better about the
seduction campaign he intended to wage on her.

She'd banned touching, teasing and question time
but she hadn't banned looking and she hadn't banned
scent.

Her bad.

The cologne collection in the en-suite cupboard gave
him a wide and varied selection to choose from. Eeeny
meeny miney mo. Catcha... That was the aim. To catch
Ruby Maguire and play a while.

Gucci it was.

Run his fingers through his hair, find some shoes, put them on. Plastic in wallet, wallet in pocket.

Damon West was ready to shop.

He found her in the atrium, positioning a delicate porcelain Santa amongst the fern fronds that banked the goldfish pond. 'There,' she said as he approached. 'The perfect spot for Santa to enjoy a little R and R.'

Ruby Maguire stood and turned his way, no comment on the suit. She probably hadn't expected anything else.

She breathed in deeply though and closed her eyes and smiled. She had the freest smile he'd ever seen.

'I love that scent on a man,' she murmured approvingly. 'Brings back fond memories.'

'Old boyfriend?'

'Grandfather,' she corrected sweetly.

This woman was so *bad* for a man's ego. Damon smiled and meant it. Nothing like a challenge.

'Ready to go?' she said next, and he nodded and watched in silence as she headed for her oversized satchel, her ballet-style slippers making no sound on the marble floor. Odd choice of shoes to be wearing with crisply tailored grey trousers and a vivid fuchsia sleeveless silk top with an embroidered panel down the front that screamed couture, but all became clear when she opened the coat cupboard beside the front door and swapped her soft slippers for strappy black sandals with a stiletto heel.

'I can't stand high heels on marble floors,' she explained. 'It's the clickety-clack. Where's the elegance? Not to mention the ability to retreat without being seen or heard. That's a very useful skill on occasion. Not, I hasten to add, that I've ever had to use that ability here. Your father doesn't womanise.' She reset the alarm before closing the cupboard door. 'It's a refreshing change.'

'Yours did?' he asked as he ushered her out of the door and closed it behind them.

'Oh, yes. It was just a game, you see. Everything from stealing another man's woman to the removal of vast sums of other people's money—it was all just a game.'

'Where was your mother in all of this?'

'Living happily in Texas with oil baron husband number three. He doesn't womanise either, come to think of it. That's *two* I know.'

'Wouldn't *he* give you a job if you asked for one?'

'Probably, but I don't work for family, Damon. Never have, never will.'

'Another rule?'

'That one's more of a survival trait. Work for family and before you know it they're trying to control your life.' They stepped into the elevator and Ruby pressed the button to the foyer. 'How loaded is your daddy's credit card when it comes to buying Christmas gifts for his children?' she asked. 'Because I happen to have it with me.'

'He bought us a plane once,' said Damon. 'We had to share it though.'

'Poor baby,' she murmured with another one of those carefree smiles that put him in mind of a kid in a sweets shop. 'Not sure I can swing another aircraft or two at such short notice, but I've absolutely no objection to shopping with the sheiks and the sugar daddies if that's the norm. The Landmark it is.'

The Landmark shopping mall butted onto the Landmark Oriental Hotel, which meant valet parking and rampant indulgence. Ruby's mode of transport, an Audi R5 in panther-black with a pearl finish, would fit right in.

'Yours?' he murmured.

'Was that a question?' asked Ruby. 'I thought we'd banned personal questions.'

'You just asked me one.'

'I asked about the cost of Christmas gifts for your family. That was business.'

'No, that's about as personal as it gets. I, on the other hand, merely questioned whether this car was yours. It could be a company car. It could be my father's, though I doubt it. His taste runs to saloons.'

'It's mine. I chose it and paid for it myself. Happy now?'

'Yes. And I heartily approve of your choice of wheels. It almost makes up for your choice of hair accessory. What *is* that thing on your head anyway?' She'd slipped it on in the car. He'd been staring at it ever since.

'It's a headband. It keeps my hair out of my face and what's more, I guarantee it'll get us taken seriously when it comes to shopping where we're shopping. You'll see.'

'Ruby, it's a frothy pink bow on a leopard-skin band.'

'No, it's high-end couture. This is serious frou-frou.'

'I have another question,' he said.

'You're wondering where the money comes from,' she said. Which he was.

'Am I really that easy to read?'

'No, it's just that it's the first question everyone asks. Feds, lawyers, strangers... Everyone wants to know if I'm spending my father's ill-gotten gains. I'm not. The money's clean. I'm a trust-fund baby, courtesy of my late grandmother.'

'So you don't actually *need* to work for my father. I could, in effect, attempt to engage your affections with a clear conscience.'

'No, you'd still be stricken with guilt—that is, if you *do* guilt. My grandmother was not one to encourage idleness. The trust is set up so that for every dollar I earn it releases two. More if I throw in a good deed or two for charity, which, as luck would have it, I do.'

'And what would your grandmother have thought of the car?'

'She'd have *loved* the car,' said Ruby, and swung out of the car park and into the Hong Kong traffic with a confidence born of insanity. 'There's a massage option built into the seat if you feel the need to relax,' she murmured as she expertly cut her way across three lanes of traffic in order to take the next right.

'I'm fine,' he squeaked, but by the time they reached the shopping mall he had renewed his acquaintance with prayer and discovered that Ruby Maguire was either totally fearless, bent on annihilation by way of traffic incident or stark-raving mad.

The shopping centre did nothing to soothe Damon's already fragile peace of mind. 'You know what you're looking for, right?' he asked a touch desperately as he glanced up at the waterfall of retail stores rimming the central atrium.

'No,' said Ruby cheerfully. 'I have no idea. That's why you're here. You can start by telling me whether your sisters are girly girls when it comes to gifts or more practically inclined? Should I be thinking handbags for Poppy or season tickets to the Royal Ballet? She lives in London, right?'

'Right. And definitely the tickets. Buying tickets online would mean we wouldn't necessarily have to go into *any* of these shops. Problem solved.'

'Or we could put the tickets *in* the handbag,' murmured Ruby. 'Or in the pocket of a black velvet evening coat. Do you have her measurements?' Damon shook his head. Ruby sighed her impatience. 'C'mon, Damon. Work with me here. Surely a rake of your stature can hazard a decent guess as to dress size? We're not going to swing tailor-made at this time of year anyway. It'll have to be ready-to-wear.'

'In that case, Poppy's five seven and too slender for her own good. Size ten, Australian.'

'Thank you. I knew you could do it. What about Lena?'

'Lena is a little taller and has spent six of the last eight months in a wheelchair. She's even skinnier than Poppy these days. I hope it doesn't last.'

'So…dress size eight? Or ten?'

'Yes,' he said and earned himself an eye roll. 'Ten would be better. Give her something to aspire to.'

'And what size am I?'

Nice of Ruby to give him permission to study her delectable form. 'Arms above your head and turn around,' he directed smoothly.

'Funny man.' Ruby's honey-coloured eyes narrowed

and her hands went to her hips. Damon's gaze followed.
Her waist was tiny but she did have hips. Not to mention
a fine rear and full breasts. Her chestnut curls stayed
clear of her face, courtesy of the ridiculous headband,
and the black leather tote completed her general air of
plenty.

Plenty of curves, plenty of attitude and plenty of
challenge to be going on with. Damon smiled his ap-
preciation.

'Somewhere between a size ten and a twelve, Ruby,
though I'm guessing most of your clothes are custom
fit. You've got that look. How am I doing so far?'

'You're a true expert on the female form. Lucky me.
Now tell me what kind of clothes your sisters prefer to
wear.'

Damon looked warily upwards once again, towards
the retail floors filled with shops. They seemed like
very spacious shops. Probably not *that* many per floor.
'Poppy likes layers. Lena hates dresses. Neither of them
are into colour.'

'That's just sad,' she murmured. 'Do they like jewellery?'

'They have jewellery.'

'I'm working on the general assumption that they
have everything,' said Ruby dryly. 'In here, Damon,'
she said, gesturing to the nearest shopfront. 'No one
does neutrals better than the French.'

Bracing himself, Damon followed her inside.

It wasn't Ruby's headband that got them exemplary
service, decided Damon a few minutes later. It was her
attitude. The way she knew not to browse the racks herself but describe what she wanted and then let the as-

sistants fetch the stuff. The way she efficiently sorted the offerings into discards and items she wanted to consider. There was seating, and Damon availed himself of it. Refreshments, which he declined.

Three saleswomen and one curvaceous general. Two presents to purchase. Five minutes, tops.

He was so wrong.

What kind of maniac put a beige trench coat over what looked like a corseted black baby-doll nightie? Or covered a perfectly serviceable strapless black mini dress with a sheer purple overgown that rippled to the floor?

The purple gauzy thing and the mini beneath it were discarded on account of Lena not being one for colour or dresses. In the end, Ruby settled on a pewter-coloured miniskirt for Lena. It had ruffles and looked softly feminine and would not emphasise his sister's frailty. Damon approved. The ivory-coloured waist-length jacket Ruby chose to go with it had some sort of sculpted band around the hem but it went with the skirt better than expected. The beige trench coat and the baby-doll nightwear combo that she'd set aside was apparently for Poppy.

'Do I get a say?' he murmured and four perfectly styled women turned to regard him with varying degrees of pity. 'You said *handbags*,' he said to Ruby mildly. 'To put the tickets in?'

'Dammit, you're right,' she said, and turned to the attendants. 'We'll need to look at handbags too. Satchels, I think.'

'In the black?' asked an attendant.

'Of course.'

Half an hour later they left the shop, goodies in hand, and with Ruby sporting the kind of glow that only came from hitting a credit card hard. 'Now you,' she said. 'Would you like a new suit?'

'Why? What's wrong with my suit?'

'Nothing.'

'Then I don't want another one.'

'How about a watch?'

'I got this one from Poppy and Lena last Christmas. I've worn it once.'

'Well, that's hardly the watch's fault,' she said with a glance at his wrist. 'It's a very nice watch. What about gadgetry? New phone? Camera? Computer? What is it that you do?'

'I troubleshoot computer systems.'

'For who?' She looked intrigued.

'For those who ask.'

'Where are you based?'

'I don't have a base. The job's portable.'

'But surely life *isn't*? Or are you one of those people who just can't seem to settle anywhere?'

'Something wrong with variety?'

'I guess not.' She didn't sound impressed. 'All right. What about a new set of travel bags for Christmas? We're in the neighbourhood.'

'There's some new computer tech I'm interested in. Why don't you leave it with me?'

'That's not what I'm paid to do, and, frankly, I hate leaving jobs undone. It's a little quirk of mine.'

'Another one.'

'Exactly.' There was that disarming smile again. Feminine weaponry at its finest. 'If I don't have a gift for you by the end of the day I won't sleep. If I don't sleep I get cranky. It's not a good look.'

'How so? Do you abandon the fuchsia headband for a schoolmarm's bun and a riding crop?' It was possible. Judging by the shop they'd just raided, anything was possible. Ruby's golden eyes narrowed. Damon offered up his own disarming smile. 'I can see that working for you.'

'I'm glad we went shopping together,' she murmured. 'You've saved me from fantasising about you later.'

'Because I'm hard to buy for? Or because I'm homeless.'

'Neither. There's something else about you that makes you a dismal relationship choice, and once again I can credit my recently departed father for giving me a heads up.'

'Sounds ominous.'

'It is. It's about deception and disguise and people who deliberately portray themselves as something they're not. You make a charming wastrel, by the way. I'm very impressed. But that's not what you are.'

'So what am I?' he asked quietly.

'Far smarter than you're letting on, for starters,' she offered bluntly. 'Beautifully evasive when it comes to talking about your work, your needs and your lifestyle choices. An old hand, I surmise, at keeping whatever passes for the real you completely hidden from view. You're not feckless, Damon. You're a liar.'

CHAPTER TWO

IT REALLY wasn't supposed to work like this, thought Damon grimly. Finally he'd encountered a woman who saw more of him than most—and granted, she had the benefit of working for his father and therefore knowing more of his family background than most women did at first glance—but still...

Wasn't she supposed to *like* what she saw of the real Damon West? Admire his complexity and want to know more, not label him a liar and a bad relationship bet along with it.

'Everybody lies, Ruby,' he protested carefully, and watched her lips twist into a bitter smile.

'Not everybody, Damon. Not to the extent that you do. Few people misrepresent themselves the way you do. Only those with something to hide. Con men, thieves, spooks. Shadow people. The ones you can never know because they never let you, and the only thing you can count on is that you'll wake up one day and they'll be gone. Who are you really, Damon? What is it that you do? Are you a money tracker? Is that why your father respects you? Are you here looking for a lead on *my* father? Because I've already told you, I don't know where he is.'

'I'm not a money tracker.'

'Then what are you? Special intelligence service like your brother and sister? What? I'm being as forthright as I know how to be. Just tell me why you're here and what you need from me. If I have it, it's yours. No seduction required. No more pretty lies. I am so *sick* of lies.'

Her eyes were like bruises and they got to him more than he cared to admit.

'I'm not SIS, and I swear—on my father's honour—that I'm not hunting your father, or the money he stole, or anything else related to him or to you. Look at me,' he commanded softly and waited until she did. 'I'm here for Christmas with my family, that's all. No hidden agenda, Ruby. None.'

'Oh, hell,' she murmured, and looked around the shopping centre, blinking fast as if holding back tears. 'I'm sorry. I thought... It felt...'

'Like you were being played. You were, but not with nefarious intent.' She'd wanted the truth from him and he gave her what he could. 'I thought you could handle yourself. I thought you could handle me. Maybe I'm not all I seem to be, I'll give you that. Maybe I'm not the kind of man Ruby Maguire needs to have around her right now. I'll give you that too. I didn't know that earlier. Now I do. No more playing with Ruby, see?' He took a careful step back to emphasise his words. 'No harm done.'

'I'm sorry, I... You must think I'm a paranoid nutter,' she muttered, setting her shopping bags down so she could slide her headband off, shake her curls free and put it back on again. Busywork for her hands while she looked anywhere but at him.

'It's not wrong to be careful of other people, Ruby. I would be too, were I in your position.' He let her collect her composure. He looked at the nearest retail store, seeking distraction and finding it. 'I'm thinking I might need some casual wear,' he offered. 'As a Christmas gift from my father to me. They sell that kind of menswear around here, right?'

'Right,' she said and took a deep breath.

'Can we bypass the polo shirts though?'

'Good call,' she murmured. 'I'm betting upscale grunge is far more you. I'm thinking jeans to start with and we'll improvise from there. How are you off for underclothes?' She rallied fast, did Ruby Maguire, and Damon's admiration for her rose a notch.

'Do they have a brand name plastered all over them?'

'Only on the band.'

'In that case, I don't want any. I prefer my underwear anonymous.'

'Of course you do,' she murmured soothingly. 'I should have guessed. Would you like any help with your clothing selection, or shall I just wait?'

'I want your help. Whatever it was you did in the other store, do that,' he added. 'Only faster.'

Half an hour later Ruby had Damon outfitted in clothes that might even find their way into his travel bag, and relative amicability had been restored. Ruby had more shopping to do but none that required Damon's assistance. Damon had more shopping to do too, and he definitely didn't need assistance. Ruby had agreed to drop him off at the Golden Computer Shopping Centre in Kowloon. Damon would find his own way back to the apartment. Too easy.

'Mind the scams,' she said as they loaded up her car with his father's purchases.

'I shall enjoy them immensely,' he murmured and she shot him a perplexed glance. 'I'm only browsing, Ruby. Seeing what's new and improved or old and abused. I do it every time I come to Hong Kong.'

'So...you really do work with computers?'

Damon nodded. Not a lie, even if it wasn't the whole truth. Ruby headed for the driver's seat. Damon to the passenger side.

'Is there any particular type of food or beverage you'd like me to stock the apartment with?' she asked as they filled the car with shopping bags and then themselves. 'Your favourites? Your sisters' favourites?'

'Lena likes a good Sauvignon Blanc, Poppy loves lychees and I'm a sucker for crispy duck in pancake pockets with all the trimmings. No one's all that keen on a-thousand-year-old eggs, shark-fin soup, turtle jelly, or chicken-feet anything.'

'Not a problem. I'll steer clear of the swallow's nest tonics and imported Japanese blowfish too. And, Damon?'

The seriousness was back in her voice.

'I'm really sorry about our earlier misunderstanding.'

'Don't be,' he said gently. 'I've forgotten it already.'

Ruby hit the grocery stores after that. White wine, fresh fruit—including lychees—and crispy duck with all the trimmings. Snack food for Russell's fridge that she took back to the apartment immediately in the hope that Damon would still be out.

He wasn't.

'You shop too fast,' she said as she downed her numerous shopping bags, opened the coat cupboard and slipped out of her high heels and into her flats. He'd taken his jacket off and rolled up his shirtsleeves.

If a sexier version of manhood existed, Ruby hadn't seen it.

'Dare I suggest that you shop too much?' he countered as he closed the door behind her and picked up the shopping bags.

Now she'd seen it.

'I smell food,' he said.

'It's crispy duck. I was going to put it in the fridge for later.'

'Ruby, you spoil me.' Damon's grin became boyishly delighted.

'It's Christmas.'

'It's great.'

Ruby watched as Damon set the bags down next to the bench and found the one with his favourite food in it. Man and his stomach. Always the same, no matter what his pay grade. 'It's still hot,' he said.

'The restaurant's only a block away. If you like the food I'll give you their number.' Ruby started on the unpacking. The sooner she did her job, the sooner she could leave. Leaving was preferable to being around Damon. Damon called forth feelings she didn't want any part of. Starting with desire for a man who kept far too many secrets. 'Pretend I'm not here,' she told him.

'But you *are* here.'

'Then think of me as the hired help.'

'Of course.' He gestured towards the takeaway containers he'd lined up on the counter. 'Want some?'

Ruby rolled her eyes and kept right on unpacking. Fruit for the fruit bowl by way of a water rinse. She found the colander and started washing grapes. A grape escaped her and rolled across the counter towards him. He stopped it, ate it, and Ruby's gaze slid helplessly to his lips.

Not good.

'Does my father treat you like an employee?' he murmured.

'Why wouldn't he?'

'Just curious.'

'Whatever you're thinking just say it,' she said darkly.

'I was thinking that I can see now why plenty of people *wouldn't* want to employ you. If there were women around you'd outclass them. Husbands around and you'd captivate them. Furthermore, I'm willing to bet that my father treats you more like a daughter than an employee.'

'I think it's because he met me a couple of times as a child. I'm trying to break him of the habit.'

'There it is,' he said softly. 'The reason you'll never make a good underling. You're too regal. Taking charge comes as automatically to you as breathing.'

'So?' For some reason his words wounded her.

'It's not a criticism, Ruby. I'm just saying that asking me to treat you like the hired help is all well and good but it's never going to happen. You're Ruby Maguire;

part princess, part seasoned survivor when it comes to the whims of the wealthy, and you know it. What's more, I know it. We're just going to have to come up with some other way of dealing with each other.'

'Are we having another serious conversation?' she demanded suspiciously. 'Because, I still remember how well the last one worked out for us.'

'You think we should stick to banter? Flirting without intent?'

'Yes,' she said firmly. 'It's the perfect solution. Easy as breathing, for both of us—no character assassination intended.'

'None taken,' he said dryly. 'Flirting is comfortable.'

'Exactly.'

'Predictable.' He seemed to be looking for a catch.

'I'm sure we can make it so.'

'Safe,' he said, watching her closely.

'Possibly a new experience for the mysterious Damon West, but yes,' she said airily. 'Flirting with me is comfortable, predictable, easy and safe.'

'Right.' Damon's enthusiasm for flirting—with or without intent—appeared to be on the wane. 'What if I fall asleep?'

'It's all right, Damon.' Hard not to smile at Damon West's thorough comprehension of self. 'I'll wake you before I leave.'

Ruby did leave Damon's company eventually, and she took with her plenty of food for thought. She'd never thought of herself in the terms that Damon West had described her. Part princess, part seasoned survivor.

Yes, she knew her way around the upper echelons of

society; with its games of one-upmanship and the ul-
timate scorecard that was money. Yes, she could relate
to being a survivor. Always had been. Another lesson
from her father. But she'd never thought of herself as
authoritative, or a princess for that matter. She'd never
considered herself a difficult woman to deal with.

Recent bouts of rampant paranoia aside.

She'd left Damon enjoying his meal and showing no
signs of resentment towards her whatsoever, in the aftermath of her accusations and suspicions. Social disas-
ter alleviated. Good for her. For her and Damon both,
given that she'd be seeing a fair bit of him over the next
few days.

The rest of Ruby's afternoon consisted of a charity
meeting on Russell's behalf, and once she'd clocked
off for the day, getting her nails done, and doing a spot
of Christmas gift shopping, this time for herself. Her
modest optic fibre Christmas tree had no gifts beneath
it. Now it would.

Ruby let herself into her own apartment shortly after
7:30 p.m. Shoes off at the door—an old habit, drummed
into her by a long-ago nanny—and a smile for the tiny
half-grown cat who peered at her suspiciously from beneath the lounge chair. The kitten had been haunting
the residents' underground car park, half starved, not
tough enough for the streets, and Ruby had been lonely.
They'd agreed on a one-week trial. Today was the start
of week three and the ribbed look had faded somewhat
but the little cat's wariness remained. 'Evening, C.'

Such a pity cats didn't talk back.

'I met a man today. A man who saw straight through
me, and I through him.'

The little cat regarded her gravely.

'That's what I thought,' murmured Ruby as she knelt, stretched out her hand and managed to touch the little cat's shoulder with her fingertips before he retreated. 'Scary stuff, but we managed a respectable distance, of sorts. Eventually. Hey, I got you a present.' Ruby dug in her grocery bag and drew out a fluffy toy mouse and set it on the floor. The cat disappeared back beneath the lounge. So much for progress.

'All righty then. How about some food?'

Ruby headed for the galley kitchen, switching on lights with her elbow as she went. She fed the cat, set soothing music to playing and put a plate of leftover stir-fried vegetables in the microwave. She poured a glass of white wine and sipped it as she crossed to the window and stared out over the vast and bustling Victoria harbour.

This job for Russell West had only ever been a stop-gap while she recovered from the blow of her father's deception. She'd made of her duties what she could, and she would *always* be grateful to Russell for giving her safe haven when others had cast her aside, but it was time to move on and Damon's observations had merely confirmed it. Domestic servitude wasn't for her. She needed to find something else to do. Start her own business. Study a different type of law. One not associated with big business and big money. Something humanitarian.

'What do you think, cat? Would I make a good human rights advocate?' Sighing, Ruby pulled her headband from her hair and tossed it on the nearby table.

'No? How about family law? Prenups. Divorce.' Given her family history she knew plenty about both.

Damon West had thought her headband ridiculous.

Damon West had thought a lot of things about her, most of them accurate. Ruby in turn just couldn't seem to stop thinking about *him*.

Whether those thoughts were accurate was anyone's guess.

'What do you reckon he is, C? A thief?'

No answer from the little cat.

'But then, Russell would hardly be proud of a thief. Maybe Damon's a legitimate thief—moral ambiguity aside. Maybe he works for one of those government agencies no one's ever heard of. Either way, we don't want any part of him, right, Cat? We don't like people who keep secrets. Secrets bite. You'd know all about bites, right?'

Ruby took another sip of wine, and breathed a lonely sigh. 'You think I should have encouraged him, don't you? Used him to get through the Christmas lonelies, and yes, he'd have been perfect for that. Then I could have handed in my notice come New Year and we'd have never had to see each other again. It could've worked beautifully.'

She turned to look at the little cat and the little cat looked back.

'I disagree,' she said solemnly and hoped like hell that her decision would stick. 'I'm lonely; Damon's solitary. There's a difference.'

The little cat miaowed and Ruby nodded her agreement. 'I know,' she said. 'It's a big difference.'

* * *

For once in his life, Damon couldn't keep his mind on the job. He'd found his way to an internet café in Kowloon and logged on to an unsecured network somewhere in the vicinity. He had his laptop with him, the hardware he'd purchased earlier that day in place, he had need of information and he had the skill required to get it without anyone noticing. The clock said 1:00 a.m. Hong Kong time but he was wide-awake. He knew the codes, most of them anyway. All he had to do was bring up the page and start the run.

Why then, instead of doing just that, was he sitting there at the shabby, semi-private computer station obsessing over his recent encounters with one Ruby Maguire? Rewriting them in his head so that they played out the way he wanted them to play out. With him the hero and Ruby suitably awed by his air of mystery and rapier wit.

Not *now*, Damon. C'mon. *Concentrate.*

Lena had asked him to look into Jared's whereabouts. She'd wanted to know if ASIS had Jared listed as active, which would mean he was on a job rather than off doing heaven only knew what on his own. Didn't mean Lena suspected anything untoward. Didn't mean Jared was neck-deep in trouble. This was just an insurance run, nothing more. To set their minds at ease.

He pulled up the website he needed, started the run and sat back and put an online gaming map up on the screen while he waited. Two minutes, he estimated. Tops.

And then the laptop beeped and Damon switched screens, noting with a frown the distinct *lack* of anything remotely resembling his brother's employment file. Not good. Time to dig deeper and hope to hell he didn't find Jared's file down in the pit with all the other dark ponies. Swiftly, Damon cut his way further into the system, cursing inwardly as what should have been a two-minute milk-run turned into a five-minute nightmare.

Six minutes, seven minutes and way past time for Damon to be getting the hell out of the files he was sifting through and still he hadn't found any information concerning his brother.

Nine minutes into the run and he found a file strung full of encrypted numbers. Heading the string was Jared's employee number. It'd have to do.

Backing out of the system without a trace took Damon past the ten-minute mark—too long for comfort, with his safety margin well and truly shot.

Pack up, get out. Take the long way home. With the adrenalin blowing through his skull and every sense he owned on hyper-alert.

Minutes later, as he stepped onto the first underground train that came along, Damon West, IT engineer and specialist systems hacker ever since he'd found his way into his high school's assessment database at the tender age of twelve, grinned.

CHAPTER THREE

DECEMBER twenty-third came hot and humid. By midafternoon there'd be a deluge, Ruby predicted. A blast from the sky to wash away the stench of the day. A deluge to avoid if at all possible, she decided as she set about ensuring that she'd stocked Russell's apartment with everything the West family could possibly want or need over the Christmas break, including provisions for unexpected guests, should any drop in.

The rainclouds were still a long way off when Ruby phoned through to Russell's apartment at midday to say she was on her way up but no one picked up, and Ruby breathed a mingled sigh of disappointment and relief.

No Damon, no temptation. This was a good thing.

Dry-cleaning over one arm, shopping bag full of sushi dangling from her fingertips and a gingerbread house balanced precariously on top of the dry-cleaning, Ruby elbowed her way through the doorway to the apartment and slipped off her shoes. No time to put her flats on because if she didn't get rid of the gingerbread house soon she'd drop it and that really wouldn't do.

'Are you ever not carting things from one place to the

next?' asked a voice from behind her and Ruby jumped and the gingerbread house started to slide.

Damon caught it well before it hit the floor and Ruby's thanks came thin and grudging, seeing as he was the one who'd startled her into dropping it in the first place. She turned to look at him, taking in his choice of clothing for the day—a white linen shirt that she hadn't seen before, and well-fitting jeans that looked decidedly familiar. The clothes looked crisp and fresh. The body beneath them seemed a little rumpled. 'I thought you were out.'

'That was you on the phone five minutes ago?'

'Yes.'

'Sorry. I was asleep. By the time I'd found the phone and picked up, you'd put down.'

'Jet lag?'

'Possibly.'

'There are tonics for that.'

'It's Hong Kong. There are tonics for everything.'

'Just a suggestion,' she murmured and started towards Russell's rooms where his suits lived. When she returned and slid the sushi into the fridge, she found the gingerbread house on the kitchen bench and a tousle-haired Damon cracking open a fizzy drink that hadn't entered the apartment by way of Ruby.

'You've been shopping,' she accused.

'Guilty.'

'If you want anything like that, let me know. That's my department.'

'Ruby, I'm quite capable of stepping out for half a dozen cans of cola. Consider it exercise and a change of scenery on my part.'

'That's really not how it works.'

'No, that's usually exactly how it works,' he murmured with a crooked smile. 'Want one?'

'Just water, please. It's slick out. Hopefully the icing hasn't slid off the roof of the house.' Ruby gave the confectionary a careful once-over but all looked well with Santa's gingerbread cottage. 'Are we flirting yet?'

'Just working my way up to it,' he said with a smiling glance in her direction. 'It's all in the timing.' He looked back at the cellophane wrapped gingerbread house. 'Anyone ever tell you that you shop too much?'

'You're the first. Speaking of shopping, are those the jeans we bought for you yesterday?'

Damon nodded. 'Useful, aren't they?'

'There goes the Christmas present,' she murmured. 'Perhaps I forgot to mention the part where I wrap them up and put them under the tree?'

'That can still be arranged,' he said dryly.

'It's not the same. You're meant to wait. Take possession on Christmas *Day*.'

'It's just another day, Ruby.'

'Well, it is *now*. Take them off.'

Grinning, Damon set his drink down and reached for his fly. Ruby raised a delicate eyebrow but made no move to stop him. Eventually he stopped of his own accord.

'You're supposed to say "not here",' he said. 'And then you blush.'

'Not sure we're living in the same universe, my friend.'

'I'll say. Good thing I'm adaptable.' The trousers came off. He handed them to Ruby, who stripped his belt from the trousers and handed it back to him with considerable expertise.

'And the rest of the clothes from yesterday,' she said airily. 'When you're ready.'

'Good thing we didn't buy underwear,' he murmured and set off up the hall, not an ounce of self-consciousness anywhere in sight. Just strong, athletic legs, broad, shirt-covered shoulders, and a hint of mighty fine buttock. Put today's picture together with yesterday's man-and-his-towel image, and a woman could be excused for losing her breath.

'I know you're looking,' he said from halfway down the hall.

'No, I'm not.' But she said it with a smile, and she leaned over the counter the better to catch the show.

Only once he'd reached his room did Ruby drag her attention away from Damon West's very fine form to study his can of cola and note the label. She'd add it to the drinks order and make sure a case of it arrived later this evening with the last of the Christmas Day fare.

When Damon returned he had the rest of the clothes they'd purchased yesterday in hand and a pair of vivid Hawaiian board shorts on person.

'A leftover from your last stint as a pool boy?' she queried delicately.

'What? You don't like them? They're my favourite.'

'Oh, Damon. That's just...' Words failed her. 'Sad.' She handed the new trousers back to him with a sigh. 'Put them back on before your father sees you. He has a reputation to maintain.'

'Ruby, you confuse me,' he murmured, but he took

hold of the trousers deftly enough and the edges of his
lips signalled his satisfaction.

'Player,' she accused.

'Despot.'

'Yes, but I'm a benevolent one. How many of these
clothes we bought you yesterday are you going to need
to wear tomorrow?'

'Only the shirt. And the jeans again. Maybe the
jacket.'

Ruby sighed, temporarily defeated. Maybe she could
shop with him in mind on the way home. Something
with a V-neck and tiny little sleeves. Flared pants with
spangles. 'Would it have killed you to get *two* sets of
clothes when we were shopping earlier?'

'I wasn't sure that shop was me.'

'There *were* other shops.'

'Yes, I know,' he said with a shudder. 'They were
everywhere. But two clothes shops a year is my limit
and we did them both yesterday.'

'We need to build your stamina.'

'I have stamina,' he murmured. 'It's selective.'

'Ah,' she murmured. 'Now we're flirting.'

'Correct.'

Ruby's gaze cut to Damon's mouth. Flirting was
meant to be light. Fun. Not deeply, emotionally satis-
fying.

Moments later those tempting lips got a great deal
closer as Damon leaned towards her in much the same
way as she had done the first time they'd met. Bench
in between them but personal space still well and truly
invaded. Her eyes moved up to meet Damon's gaze and

there was a promise there waiting for her, and a challenge if she dared to accept it.

'Something you want from me, Ruby?' he asked silkily.

'Nope. Definitely not. Can't think of anything. At all.'

'Liar,' he whispered softly.

'Are you sure this is flirting without intent?' she whispered back.

'Now that you mention it, I may have acquired intent,' he murmured.

'That's really not part of the plan.'

'I know.' He rocked forward until his lips brushed hers. 'The plan was flawed. No pep.'

'Don't you have cola for that?'

'It's not enough.'

'Is that a favourite saying of yours?'

'It is of late.' He touched his lips to hers again and his big body grew very still. Warm lips against her own and a bench in between them as he waited for her response.

Time seemed to stop as Ruby battled for control of her wayward reaction to Damon West. Not flirty and easy but complex and needy. So much need in her to taste the essence of this man.

Tentatively, she set the tip of her tongue to one corner of his lips and tested the seam. In. He let her in, and he tasted of sweetness and his tongue knew how to tease, drawing her deeper into passionate play, and he led and she followed, and then she led and he let her.

Lightness of touch and an homage to languor and beneath it all a deep well of scorching heat. Ruby backed out of the kiss reluctantly, before it consumed her, and Damon moaned his protest and took one last fast taste before letting her pull back.

'God, we'd be good in bed together,' he rumbled and turned away and headed for the fridge.

Ruby closed her eyes and offered up a silent prayer. Dear God, not this one. *Please*, not this one, for his capacity to enchant was too high, and the likelihood of him giving much of himself seemed alarmingly low.

When Damon returned from his foray in the fridge, he had a bowl of ice cubes and a tin of caviar. The ice-bowl went between them on the counter and the caviar got upended on top of it. Next, he opened a packet of breadsticks and set it next to the rest.

'Eat,' he said. 'And remind me again why you're not going to sleep with me, apart from the fact that you work for my father, need to keep your job and consider me a habitual liar. I don't know about you, but it doesn't seem enough.'

Rather than answer, Ruby sampled the food on offer. A pause where pause was needed. An ice cube topped with caviar, and a cool and salty slide. She crunched down on the ice and let the textures mingle. 'Mmm.' Good manners prevented speech, so another *mmm* would have to be enough.

'Good, isn't it? Much like we'd be.' Sighing, Damon picked up a breadstick, loaded it with eggs and held it to her lips. 'The caviar usually runs out before the ice does. Say *aah*.'

'Ahumm.' The breadstick went in loaded and came out clean. A husky oath filled the air.

Damon's.

'Give me a reason not to, Ruby,' and his voice came low and guttural and slid down her spine like a lover's hand. 'Give me a reason to back off, or I swear I'll be inside of you before the day is through.'

Ruby swallowed hard and attempted to marshal her thoughts. 'I work for your father,' she said weakly.

'Not good enough.'

'I'll lose my job.'

'Says who?'

'I don't know you.'

'Would you like to?'

'Would you let me?' Finally an objection she could follow through on. 'Can you answer even the most casual of questions honestly?'

'I can try.'

'All right. Where were you this time last week? What were you doing? Just the briefest details of your day—that's all I'm asking for.'

She saw him shut down. Watched his eyes as he sifted back through time, closing compartments as he went. Not that. Not that. Can't tell her that; and his reasons for not telling her were his own. He didn't even offer up an excuse.

'Okay, different question,' she said. 'Where will you be in a week's time? Snapshot that day.'

But he couldn't seem to do that either.

'Most people would be able to answer those questions, Damon,' she said quietly. 'But then, you're not most people, are you? I may have been wrong about you being after my father, but I wasn't wrong about the rest of it. About the way you keep the details of your life to yourself. About there being so much of you that you cannot, or will not, share. Not with strangers. Not with anyone.'

Finally he swore. One word.

Not something they'd be doing anytime soon.

'Glad we cleared that up,' she said carefully, no flirting in her now, just a pitiful and aching need for something that had never been on offer. 'I need honesty from a lover, Damon. I need to taste the truth in you, even if all we'd be doing is having mindless, no-strings-attached sex. It's a requirement of mine.' She dredged up a smile from somewhere.

'Make an exception,' he cajoled gruffly. 'For me.' Nothing like the penetrating gaze of a powerfully persuasive man to make a woman's mind waver. 'I hear what you're saying, Ruby. I swear I will not lie to you. Ever. I'll just...'

'Not answer,' she finished for him softly. 'I know how it works, Damon. And for what it's worth you tempt me. So much. But what you're offering...it's not enough.'

Damon stayed broodingly silent.

'I should go,' she said awkwardly, and then as reality intruded, 'I need to do the birds first.'

'I'll do them.'

'Thank you.' Ruby made it to the door and into her shoes before job necessities made her turn to Damon once more. 'I've arranged to collect Poppy from the airport at three and bring her here.'

'I'll get her.'

'Lena gets in at six.'

'I'll get her too.'

This time Ruby managed to make it through the

doorway, shutting the apartment door behind her with a quiet click. She drew a shuddering breath and closed her eyes briefly, before putting one foot determinedly in front of the other as she headed for the lift.

He wanted too much from her. Too much for too little.

There was nothing left to say.

CHAPTER FOUR

HEATSTROKE and insanity. That was what Ruby attributed those scorching kisses to. It was hot. She was insane. Simple.

Exactly what Damon West was, apart from obsessively secretive, was still open to interpretation.

Nothing but a memory, she told herself sternly. That was what she needed him to be. A vivid and beautiful memory that a woman could look to every so often. A memory to accompany a wistful sigh, a tiny half-smile and a harmless game of what-if.

What if he had been that little bit more open with her?

What if she'd made an exception for him?

Ruby had the feeling that, in the years to come, quite a nice little fantasy would follow on from those particular thoughts. Some of the pleasure and none of the pain. Bargain.

But there was no bargain to be had in her encounter with him today. Just heaviness and no small measure of regret.

With the day split wide-open and no work to fill it with, Ruby headed back to the office. To the desk she didn't deserve and the job that took her two hours a day to do, when she was being paid for eight.

'Is Russell in?' she asked Bea, Russell's proper PA—the one with her finger on the pulse of his business commitments, not his social ones.

Bea nodded, and briefly lifted her gaze from the computer screen to favour Ruby with a laserlike stare. Bea was—without a doubt—ten times more imposing than Russell could ever hope to be. Not that anyone mentioned it.

'Is he free?'

Another nod and a half-smile this time. 'Go on in.'

Russell West did not cut a particularly fatherly figure, never mind that his hair was grey and the creases on his face had been there a while. He did cut an authoritative figure. 'Russell, may I have a moment?'

'What can I do for you, Ruby?'

'You can accept my resignation.' One didn't beat around the bush with Russell West. Time was money. A great deal of money. 'I'd like to finish up in the New Year, once we get your major social commitments out of the way.'

'You mean the Chinese New Year?'

'Nice try. I mean mid-January.'

'Why?' Russell leaned back in his chair, trusting his imposing office surroundings to work to his advantage, which they probably would have had she not been in and out of offices just as grand as this one all her life.

'Bottom line? The job's not big enough. I feel like I'm taking money for nothing.'

'The company's profit margin has gone up thirty-six per cent since you signed on, Ruby. That's hardly nothing.'

'Your social networking strategy needed some work, that's all. But that was always going to be more of a consultant's gig than an ongoing role. My work here is done. Nowadays, I'm just filling in time.'

'You're welcome to stay on, Ruby. You know that.'

'I do know that.' She smiled fondly at the older man. 'And I can't thank you enough for giving me work when I needed it. When no one else would. But I want to see if there's still room for me in the world of law. Even if I have to work gratis for a while until I get the necessary accreditation and experience to go into a particular field. There's family law. International law. Defence law. Fields where my father's supposed transgressions won't—or shouldn't—reflect back on me. After that, I'll look towards establishing my own business. It's a solid plan, don't you think?'

'Well, it's a solid thought,' he said dryly. 'I wouldn't exactly call it a plan. Generally a plan requires details.'

'I'm working on it,' she said simply.

'Do you need start-up capital?'

'Are you offering it?'

Russell steepled his hands, and regarded her thoughtfully. 'Yes.'

'Just like that?'

'Yes.'

'Because of your former friendship with my father?'

'Because I have every confidence in Ruby Maguire's ability to succeed.'

'Oh.' Suddenly Ruby's big-girl voice deserted her. 'You're very kind.'

'I prefer to use the word *astute*. Okay, Ruby, resignation accepted. Let Bea know when you want to finish up. And, Ruby, I realise it's late notice but I do hope you'll join me and my family for a meal over this Christmas break. Say, tomorrow night or even Christmas Day if you prefer?'

'Russell, thank you, but—'

'Christmas is a time for family, I agree,' he interrupted gruffly. 'But when family isn't around you make do. You've already met Damon, and I've no doubt the girls will enjoy your company. Try making do with us.'

'I—'

'Make it Christmas Eve? That way you can join us at the restaurant. You booked for five people, didn't you?'

'Yes, but—'

'We'll swing by your apartment and pick you up at quarter to seven.'

'No, I—'

But Russell and steamroller tactics were old friends. 'Excellent,' he said and offered up a small smile. 'Join us, Ruby. There's plenty of room at our table. We have family missing this year too.'

Damon met Poppy at the arrival gate and together they hit an airport bar and settled down to wait for Lena. No point dropping Poppy off at the apartment, according to Poppy, and, seeing as it was Poppy's jet lag they were juggling, Damon went with whatever made his sister happy. A bottle of mineral water and an order of mini spring rolls would hold them. A chance to talk to Poppy alone wouldn't hurt either.

'Have you heard from Jared?' she wanted to know

as they settled into the comfiest seats they could find, and Damon watched a little bit of the light go out of his sister's eyes when he answered no.

'Do you know where he is?' she said next. Different question altogether.

'Not yet, but I think Lena was right and that Jared's working a job for someone in ASIS. I found a three-month-old file that has Jared's employee number embedded in it but other than that it's fully encrypted. It needs translating. Or decoding. Possibly both. Want to give it a shot?'

'Of course.'

'It's probably not a piece of paper you want to go waving around the corridors of Academia.'

'I gathered that,' she said lightly.

'It's probably not something you'd want to trust *anyone* with.'

Poppy propped her elbow on the table and her chin in her hand. 'You really don't want to give it to me, do you?'

'I really don't.' It went against every instinct Damon possessed to drag Poppy into his world of subterfuge and secrets. 'And don't trust computers. Even yours.'

'Are you always this paranoid?'

'I'm entitled.' Damon sipped his wine and considered his words. 'This one's playing out a little too close to home for comfort, Poppy. We don't want to draw attention to ourselves. We don't know what Jared's got himself into, or who's running him. Time to be careful.'

'I'll be careful,' said Poppy quietly.

By the time Lena's plane touched down humour had

been restored and Damon and Poppy had vacated the
bar in favour of waiting for Lena at the arrival gates.

When Lena did finally emerge, she did it from a customs side door, meaning that customs had processed her
separately, and she walked with the aid of a stick and
the speed of a ninety-year-old. Her once gamine face
now looked gaunt and the glaze in her eyes told him that
pain ruled her these days. An airport employee walked
beside her, towing a suitcase, and the relief on his face
as Lena spotted them and waved was palpable.

So much for the full recovery Lena had been spouting about over the phone for the past two weeks.

'Miss West preferred not to avail herself of our
wheelchair services,' said the airport employee, and
with an almost-salute and a harried smile he handed
the luggage off to Damon and disappeared back the
way he'd come.

'Told you I could walk,' said Lena into the silence
that followed, and Damon drew her silently into his
arms for a hug, horrified anew by his sister's frailty and
the quiet terror he saw in Poppy's eyes as she stared at
her sister.

'You look wonderful,' said Lena as Damon released
her. 'Both of you. It's so good to see you.'

More 'you look wonderfuls' and none of them true,
followed by 'how was your flight?' and then came the
question Damon really didn't want to answer. 'Have
you heard from Jared?'

'No,' he murmured. 'Nothing.'

'Did you look into finding him?'

'Yeah,' he said gruffly, and with a warning glance
at Poppy. 'Nothing yet.'

Poppy picked up on his silent cue and didn't add to the conversation, but he could tell by her frown that they'd be discussing what to tell Lena and what not to tell her later. *Nothing* being Damon's preference by far.

'I'll bring the car around,' he said and nodded towards the nearest door and fled with the luggage before either of his sisters could stop him. He didn't cope well with the battering Lena had taken. He couldn't look at her without remembering just how close they'd come to losing her, and if he knew his response was childish and unhelpful, well…Jared's had been worse.

Jared had damn near lost his mind when the doctor had told them that if Lena lived, chances were she wouldn't be able to walk.

Lena had been under Jared's command when she'd been injured—a simple recon of a suspected biological weapons lab in East Timor had gone badly wrong. The last thing Lena remembered was heavy crossfire, sticky blood, and lying in the dirt and looking up at the sky. God only knew what Jared remembered about the way things had gone down, or what he held himself responsible for.

Jared had haunted the hospital until Lena had regained consciousness. He'd told Lena that the mission had been compromised from the start and that he had some business to attend to. He'd told her he'd be back as soon as he could.

That had been six months ago.

Damn right 'Have you heard from Jared?' was the first question everyone in this family asked.

* * *

Supper that evening had a festive note to it, thanks in no small measure to Ruby Maguire's pampering.

A tree had appeared in the atrium. A fibre-optic plastic fantastic, with a scattering of perfectly wrapped presents beneath—including one for him from his father that Damon knew full well meant that Ruby had shopped again for him on his father's behalf.

The tree should have looked gaudy but dim the regular lights and set it to shining and it looked magical instead. Fine wine filled the wine chiller and the light supper fare Russell pulled from the fridge found immediate favour with the girls.

'Dad, is there something you're not telling us?' asked Lena from her perch on the sofa as Poppy beat an unhurried path to the bar, poured two glasses of wine and took one over to Lena with low-key grace and unobtrusiveness. 'Supper is perfect, Poppy's just handed me a glass of my favourite white, there are fresh flowers everywhere, and are those *fairy* lights out on the terrace? They are, aren't they? I'm sensing a woman's touch. And not just a housekeeper.'

'Ruby's been in,' said Russell, offhand, and Damon smothered a grin as Lena tried to digest that little snippet without giving in to rampant curiosity.

'Ruby's Dad's social planner,' Damon murmured helpfully.

'His what?'

'She's doing Christmas for him,' he added, unable to resist winding his sister up just that little bit more.

'Ruby's the daughter of an old colleague of mine,' said Russell evenly. 'She needed a job. I gave her one.

You'll meet her tomorrow. I've invited her to dine with us.'

'As your…companion?' asked Poppy delicately as she handed their father a G and T and dangled a beer in front of Damon. A beer Damon ignored, so intent was he on hearing his father's reply.

'Ruby's younger than you are, Poppet. Credit an old man with some sense.'

Poppy wiggled the beer in front of Damon's face. Damon took it and remembered how to breathe.

'So why is she joining us for dinner?' asked Lena.

'Ruby's on her own this Christmas due to…unfore-seen circumstances,' said Russell. 'I thought you'd enjoy her company and she yours. Damon's met her.'

Yes, he had. And he hadn't exactly come away un-scathed.

His sisters were eyeing him speculatively. 'What?' he asked warily.

'What's she like?' asked Lena.

'Organised.' And because he knew his sisters well enough to know that they'd be wanting more, he added, 'Confident.'

'Attractive?' asked Poppy.

'I guess,' he muttered and watched in dismay as Poppy and Lena exchanged glances.

'What?'

'He likes her,' said Lena.

'Yeah, I'm getting that too,' murmured Poppy.

'How?' he wanted to know. 'How could you possibly get that from this conversation?'

'Instinct,' said Lena sagely.

'Not exactly an accurate science,' he countered.

Poppy just smiled.

'So what was Ruby before she became a Christmas elf?' asked Lena. 'A stranded socialite?'

'A corporate lawyer,' said his father. 'She'll go back to practising some form of law soon, I believe. Just not corporate.'

'Why not corporate?' asked Lena.

'Why not ask her yourself?' Damon murmured and earned another set of curious glances for his efforts. So much easier to dissect someone else's life as opposed to examining one's own. 'Alternatively, don't be nosy.'

'He knows,' Lena said to her sister.

'Yep,' agreed Poppy.

'All I'm saying is that everyone's entitled to their secrets,' offered Damon. 'Why not let Ruby keep hers?'

'He *really* likes her,' said Lena, staring at him in amazement.

Poppy just looked at him and smiled her gentle smile.

Ruby prepared for dinner with Russell West and his family on Christmas Eve with a great many misgivings, most of them centred around seeing Damon again. She toyed with the idea of phoning Russell and pleading ill for the evening. Lies were useful, at times. Everybody lied.

Except she'd made honesty her platform when it came to dealing with Damon West, and how could she demand something from him that she wasn't prepared to give?

Opening up her wardrobe at 5:00 p.m. with almost two hours to go until pick-up gave some indication of her state of apprehension. The restaurant encouraged formal evening wear. Suits for the gentlemen, couture for the ladies. What would Poppy and Lena be wearing? Not colours, if Damon could be believed, and in this he probably could.

'What'll I wear, C?' she asked the little tortoiseshell beast who hovered in the doorway behind her, hedging his bets as to whether he would come into the room or stay out. 'Little black dress?' She pulled two from her cupboard, one strapless and fitted, the other one more modest but still fitted. Not really one for hiding her curves, Ruby. Curves were assets and assets worked best when seen.

'Too bleak for a Christmas dinner? I agree. What about the purple? Gorgeous cut, not too daring *and* there's a matching headband. Damon's going to love that. It'll give him something external to focus on, as opposed to worming his way inside my head and digging around. Excellent idea.'

Showering and dressing for dinner didn't take Ruby long. Six o'clock arrived, bringing with it yet another bundle of nerves for her to carry to the dinner table. Six-fifteen arrived and Ruby's patience with waiting and stewing, and stewing and waiting, ran out.

She rang Russell and told him she had a few errands to see to and that she would meet them at the restaurant at seven, no need for anyone to pick her up. Russell agreed and Ruby breathed a sigh of relief because arriving separately gave her mobility and options when it came to ending the evening on her terms.

'Win for Ruby,' she told the little cat when she got off the phone. 'Russell must have been distracted.'

At exactly 7:00 p.m., Ruby walked into the restaurant

to find the Wests taking possession of narrow flutes of champagne in the pre-dinner area. They made a pretty picture, all of them together, although the family resemblance was not that strong. Damon had black hair and so did Lena. Poppy's hair was a honey-blonde colour, and Russell's had salted to grey.

Poppy had cornflower-blue eyes and a touch of fairy in her, thought Ruby fancifully. Lena's eye colour tended more towards greyscale than blue and conjured up a touch of the devil. Different souls altogether, these two, but their smiles had a similar shape to them, and their voices—as they greeted Ruby politely—had a velvet musical quality to them that delighted the ear.

Lena wore slimline black trousers and a cream-coloured camisole that served only to emphasise her pallor and her fragility. Poppy fared better in a midnight-blue and silver A-line dress and a pretty pair of strappy silver sandals. Heaven only knew what they thought of Ruby's choice of apparel for the evening, but she could probably hazard a guess. Too theatrical, way too bright...

Wonder what else they didn't have in common?

And then Ruby turned to Damon and shouldered the impact of him dressed in crisp evening wear with as much panache as she could. A wry smile for him alone, and a promise to herself not to make this evening any more difficult than it already was. Be polite. Don't get personal. Keep her fascination for this man to herself. 'Damon.'

'Ruby.' How would he play this, for they hadn't exactly parted on the best of terms? Cool and distant? Politely dismissive? What? All he had to do was give

her a clue and she would follow his lead. 'Nice headband.'

Was he...*teasing* her?

'Thank you.' This one had a chiffon butterfly
perched above her left ear. 'Not too plain?'

'Not at all.' A twitch of his lips. 'It's very festive.'

'Well, I try.' A swift glance down at his elegant charcoal tie, white shirt and charcoal suit, followed by the
arch of her eyebrow told him exactly what she thought
of his attempts at brightening up a person's day.

Damon's smile widened and Ruby felt herself relax,
just a little. She turned back to Lena to find the other
woman getting rid of a grin but leaning rather heavily
on her cane. 'I'm sorry to have kept you all waiting,'
she said. 'I hear the dining experience here is superb.
Shall we take the champagne in and be seated?'

That took time, and ordering the meals took more.
Conversation flowed around food likes and dislikes,
and how long Ruby had been living in Hong Kong,
and what she liked best about the expat lifestyle. From
there it moved on to people's favourite places around
the globe, a conversation even Poppy joined in, albeit
shyly.

Social lubrication—Ruby was good at it, she'd been
tutored by the best. But she'd been tutored in leading
a conversation, not letting it ebb and flow at will. Get
so-and-so to talk about this, her father would say, and
sometimes he'd simply been training her and sometimes
he'd been after information. Not a skill she wanted to
employ at this table.

Don't lead. It was her second motto for the evening,
right up there behind don't drool on Damon.

She managed to avoid both for quite some time. Right up until Russell mentioned that she'd soon be leaving his employ and Damon speared her with a glittering sapphire gaze.

'Why?' he wanted to know curtly, all pretence of social distance shattered.

'I want to get back to practising some kind of law,' Ruby offered carefully. Nothing to do with Damon, or what had transpired between them; she needed him to know that. 'I've been thinking about it for a while now. And then a remark someone made to me recently about my particular skill set cemented the notion that maybe I shouldn't have given up on a law career quite so quickly. You know how it is.' She smiled a quick smile. 'Sometimes it takes a stranger with a fresh eye to point out the obvious.'

'Will you stay in Hong Kong?' Another Damon question.

'There's no pressing need to stay here, no,' murmured Ruby. An answer Damon would probably find hypocritical given her fully voiced views on his inability to settle in any one place. 'I might try Geneva.'

'Are you interested in humanitarian law?' asked Poppy tentatively.

'Maybe. It's worth exploring as an option, at any rate. I'd need to retrain. Not that that's a problem.'

Ruby glanced at Damon and found him staring at her as if perplexed, and then his gaze cut to her choice of hair accessory as if that perplexed him even more. 'It's just a headband, Damon. A festive touch for a festive occasion. It doesn't define me.'

'I noticed that,' he countered quietly and held her

gaze, and Ruby cursed herself for her oversensitivity
when it came to what this man thought of her, and for
revealing that sensitivity to him and everyone else at
this table.

Time to reach for her wine and shut her mouth and
hope that someone else's manners would prevail when
clearly hers had not.

'Geneva's a pleasant city,' said Damon as a waiter appeared from nowhere to top up everyone's wineglasses.
'I was there this time last week, on my way through
from a job in Brussels. Catching up with an old employer.'

Damon didn't look at her as he delivered his words.
He didn't look at anyone, just locked his gaze on the
entreé another waiter placed in front of him and kept
it there. 'He took me on a backdoor tour through the
Palace of Nations. I recommend it.'

Ruby wasn't the only one who stared at him in astonishment. Both Lena and Poppy were gaping at him
too.

Where to begin? What to pick up on? What to leave
the hell alone?

'Huh,' said Lena, amazement running deeply through
that one incautious sound.

Ruby couldn't even manage that.

'You didn't tell me you were in Brussels?' said
Poppy, and her voice held disappointment and sorrow
rather than amazement. 'We could have met up somewhere. Oxford's not *that* far away.'

'Sorry, Poppy.' Damon shot Poppy a guarded glance.
'You know I don't do family when I'm working.'

What the hell did Damon West *do* for a living that he had to eschew his family while he was doing it?

But Damon didn't say and Ruby sure as hell didn't ask. She just looked at him and Damon looked back, his bleak gaze meeting hers, and there was no smile in them, no invitation, just a man who knew he'd said too much already and had to shut it down before he came unstuck completely.

'Pretty place, Brussels,' she said, in a weak attempt to halt the growing silence. 'It's probably my favourite city centre of all the European cities. Not too big or overwhelming.' Unlike, say, Damon's attempt at openness and transparency. 'And then there's the chocolate.'

'And the waffles,' said Lena, joining the rescue party. 'And the beer.'

'Cherry beer,' said Ruby.

'Trappist beer,' said Lena, and with a gamine grin, 'Warm beer. Something for everyone.'

'Indeed.' Ruby could come to like Lena. A lot. 'Damon, what did you like best about Brussels?' Keeping it casual, forcing a direction, and to hell with letting the conversation find its own ebb and flow. Ruby had the helm now, and she was keeping it.

'The history,' he said, and talk turned to the fields of Flanders and the hallmarks of war.

Wine flowed and the food was indeed superb. Conversation flowed too, and turned to future endeavours. To Lena hoping to build her strength and get back to work, and Poppy, who couldn't decide whether to learn Korean or study Mayan script, and to Russell, who wanted to expand his banking services into Shanghai.

No one asked Damon what lay on his horizon and he didn't say.

Washington, DC, perhaps? Maybe some other old employer would whiz him through the White House in their spare time?

Dessert was worth waiting for, and then it was time for Ruby to thank Russell for the marvellous meal, wish them all a Merry Christmas and see herself home.

She thought she'd executed a clean getaway as Damon rose to pull out her chair.

Until Russell insisted on everyone heading to the hotel foyer together, presumably so they could see her into a taxi, only by the time they got there Russell had rearranged events to his liking, in that everyone could fit in the limo, and his chauffeur would drive everyone home.

Ruby knew when to cut her losses and go with a superior plan, only by the time they arrived at Russell's high rise the plan had changed again.

Ruby didn't even see it coming until Russell alighted and helped Lena and Poppy from the car, and then leaned back down and asked Damon to see Ruby home, and by then the limo door was closing, and the limo— with her and Damon in it—was pulling smoothly away from the kerb.

'Old fox. He planned that,' she murmured, and Damon responded with a smile. 'And you let him.'

'My father has a chivalrous streak,' countered Damon. 'Surely you know that by now.'

She did know that. 'And you? What kind of streak do you have?'

'Right now I'm going to have to go with masochistic,'

he said with a twist of his lips as he leaned his head back against the black leather interior of the limo. Had Damon known how intimate this ride would be with the others gone and just the two of them in here now?

And then he turned his head towards her and the seat space she'd made sure to put between them seemed to disappear. 'I tried to answer your question,' he said quietly.

'I know.' And in doing so he'd got to her. Again. 'Did you think it would get you into my bed?'

'Not really, no.'

'Then why do it?'

'Maybe I just wanted to know what it felt like to be that open.'

'And what did it feel like?'

'Wrong.'

They lapsed into silence again, a brooding, swirling silence that complemented the black leather seats and the cavernous limo interior. Ruby rested her head back against the seat and closed her eyes against the pull of him. She'd wanted honesty from him. She hadn't realised just how much it would hurt.

'Maybe it'll get easier,' she offered quietly. 'Maybe you just need to find the right person.'

'Maybe.' But the word held a world of defeat in it, and Ruby opened weary eyes and turned her head and held his gaze.

She edged a little closer, moving slowly. It was the only way she knew to approach such a wild and wary thing. He didn't move towards her, but he didn't move away. Just watched in silence and when she set gentle lips to his he shuddered in silence too, before pulling slowly away.

'What was that for?' he whispered.

'That was for you. For trying, because I asked you to, even if it didn't go so well. Consider it my Thank You.'

'Oh.'

This time he was the one to initiate the meeting of lips, and although he had no way with words he knew exactly how to pour emotion into a kiss. Longing and regret and she knew he still wanted her in spite of his inability to be open with her, and it made her want to cry.

'That was You're Welcome,' he whispered.

And then he kissed her again and she wound her arms around his neck and his hands were gentle on her waist as he drew her onto him, over him, and pressing up into her with a sensuality she'd always known he commanded.

Not just kisses any more but the slide of her body against his and the rapid beating of his heart beneath her hand. He had a connoisseur's touch and she had a powerful need for that touch tonight. Did it really matter that she knew next to nothing about him and probably never would? She knew he wanted her—wasn't that enough?

Passion fed and passion burned as their kisses grew deeper and more urgent, and when the limo started to slow and Ruby looked out of the window through glazed eyes and saw her high rise up ahead she groaned, and Damon groaned with her.

'Drive with me a while,' he whispered, and she knew

what he was asking and she'd resisted him before but there was no resisting him now.

Slowly, she lifted her hand to her headband and slid it from her head and dropped it to the floor. 'Yes.'

Damon reached for the intercom switch and said, 'Take us for a drive,' and the limo moved off.

Time enough now to loosen Damon's tie, and the buttons on his shirt, with her forehead pressed to his and their breath mingling as he slid the straps of her dress down her arms with gentle fingers.

'Tell me you know what you're getting us into,' he muttered. 'Tell me you know what you're doing.'

'I know what I'm doing.' While the top of her dress peeled away from her body and she drew his head down to the curve of her breast. 'So do you.' As her strapless bra came apart beneath his fingers and he claimed her nipple with his lips and set her to arching back and biting her own.

He explored every hollow and worshipped every curve and before too many minutes had passed he had her beneath him on the seat, half naked and wholly mindless as he moved inside her, every stroke a revelation.

'Tell me you can taste the truth in this,' he whispered. 'In me.'

'I do taste it.'

In the way he savoured her, honoured her, and in the way his touch made her tremble.

'Tell me you won't regret this.'

'Never. Damon, not ever.'

As the driver kept driving and Ruby and Damon got lost in each other.

* * *

It had to end eventually. Love-making always had to end. With Ruby climaxing in Damon's arms as he emptied himself into her. With Damon swallowing her cries of completion and groaning softly as her body grew boneless and his did too, and somehow she ended up stretched out on top of him, with Damon's arms around her waist keeping her there.

The interior of the limo looked like someone's messy closet. Her clothes would be here somewhere and she would get around to putting them back on soon.

But not just yet.

'That was…' Damon didn't seem to know how to finish the sentence '…a revelation.'

'I concur.' Ruby pushed herself up into a sitting position, still straddling him, still very, very naked. Damon's gaze fell to her breasts and his lazy grin turned lopsided.

'Here's a tip,' he said huskily. 'If you ever want to win an argument with me, just get naked.'

'Something to remember,' she murmured. 'Are we going to argue now?'

'No.' He slid his hand around the back of her neck and rose up to kiss the side of her mouth. He wasn't done with her yet, and the notion delighted her. 'Not right now.'

She couldn't seem to get enough of his touch. Of his kisses. 'So what shall we do?'

'Ladies' choice.' He leaned back against the seat, his slitted gaze not leaving her face as he began to harden against her once more.

'Good. Because, right now I just want to sit back and enjoy the ride.'

* * *

They found their clothes and put them on eventually. They made it back to Ruby's apartment building, and it was after one, and technically Christmas Day already, and Damon had places to be—like with his family— and Ruby had things to do, like go inside and figure out what she was going to do with Damon West for the rest of the undoubtedly short time he would be around.

He was as dishevelled as Ruby, but he got out of the car when it stopped at her door, and extended his hand for hers and brought it to his lips as she alighted from the limo with most everything in place, including her headband.

'Merry Christmas, Ruby.'

'You too,' she murmured, and took her hand back and headed quickly for the door before she turned around and held out her hand for him to join her. Only when she was safely inside the foyer and heading for the lifts did she look back and smile at what she saw.

Damon, leaning against the car with his hands in his pockets as he watched her retreat, and secrets or not she knew more of him now and she had not met with disappointment.

He didn't want true intimacy from her, and a wise woman accepted the things she could not change.

A wise woman took the gift of passion and pleasure that he *had* given her and cherished them for what they were.

Best Christmas present ever.

Damon West had as much self-awareness as the next man. He knew what he was good at, and seduction was one of those things. He knew what derailed him, and commitments of the personal kind headed that list. He'd set foot on the hackers' path at the tender age of twelve when he'd hacked into his school's academic database. At seventeen—with five more schools under his belt—he'd blitzed his exams, hacked the filter the department of education used to expose students of interest, and MIT had come knocking. He'd hacked into their system too and they'd sent him back a six-page mathematical proof of his predictability and offered him an education.

That education, and the one that had followed, had given him travel, a reason for being, and all the excitement he could handle and then some. All they'd asked from him in return was absolute discretion and a willingness to go anywhere, any time.

At twenty, he thought he'd found heaven.

At twenty-five he knew he had.

He would be thirty-three in January and as he headed back to his father's apartment with the scent of Ruby Maguire on his skin and the image of her naked and open for him dominating his mind, Damon West took the time to mourn the loss of the ordinary lifestyle he'd so willingly given up.

CHAPTER FIVE

CHRISTMAS Day started late for Ruby. Nowhere to be, no reason to get up. The two gifts beneath her tiny tree were ones she'd put there herself. A book on humanitarian imperialism—that one was supposedly from the cat. The other was a bottle of her favourite perfume. A light and woodsy scent to lift the spirits and brighten the day.

A Merry Christmas phone call came in from her mother before Ruby had found her way out of her sleepwear. A mother who sounded happy and content and who urged Ruby to come and stay a while in the New Year. A mother who asked if the courier had arrived yet, and sighed her exasperation when Ruby said not.

Ruby promised to ring back when they had.

A sashimi breakfast feast for a contented little cat followed. Freshly brewed coffee for Ruby and a butter croissant with fig and honey jam got her positively cheerful. The gourmet food hamper and the ridiculous peacock-feathered hair comb from her mother made her smile. *Shoulders back, Ruby,* she could hear her mother saying. *Chin up, there's my pretty girl.*

It had been very important to her mother that Ruby be a pretty girl.

Her father had been the one to encourage her to use her brains.

Ruby's mother had wanted to share custody of their only child once divorce had been imminent but, for reasons known only to him, Harry Maguire had been having none of that.

In the end Ruby's mother had taken the settlement money and run, leaving her daughter behind with the promise that she was always just a phone call away.

Better than nothing.

Better than a laughing, smiling father who'd disappeared one day without a word but plenty of money to be going on with.

Ruby had bought him a set of pewter chess pieces for Christmas this year—how stupid was that? The gaily wrapped parcel was burning a hole through the shelf in her bedroom closet and the child in her remained hopeful that her father would contact her today. The child in her would doubtless wait all day for her charming, laughing father to arrive.

Foolish Ruby.

Only a silly, hopeful child would put on a pretty azure sun frock and blow-dry her hair and pin it back with a peacock-feathered comb and make sure she had her father's favourite Scotch on hand and his favourite food in the fridge, and then sit on the lounge reading her book while she waited for Godot to arrive.

Part of her *knew* he wouldn't come.

But another part waited and waited some more.

The day loomed empty ahead of her, with nothing to do except wonder whether Poppy and Lena had liked their gifts and whether Damon liked his.

She'd shopped again on his father's behalf seeing as he'd taken to wearing the clothes they'd bought the other day. A lightweight travel bag that would be useless to anyone with more than a single change of clothes, and in one compartment she'd added a couple of pairs of the plainest no-name underwear she could find, and in the main compartment she'd placed a Panama hat. Everything the modern happy wanderer would ever need.

It was Lena who phoned through to thank Ruby for her gift-buying efforts, but it was Damon who got hold of the phone after that.

'Merry Christmas, Ruby.' Damon's voice came through smoothly polite. 'Your touch is everywhere here today—and we wanted to thank you for it.'

'Have the caterers been in?'

'In and gone, with a week's worth of leftovers in the fridge,' said Damon. 'Which is no reflection whatsoever on the quality of the food. The food was fantastic.'

'And your sisters liked the clothes?'

'They did. Now Lena's heading to her room for a nap, my father's heading to the study to disguise his nap as a work effort, Poppy's just started watching *It's A Wonderful Life* and I'm about to head out for a while.'

'Where?'

'Anywhere. Why? You looking for something to do?'

'What, and miss out on *It's A Wonderful Life*?'

'How many times have you seen it before? Trust me, you know how it goes. Downtrodden man reflects on his life, realises how many people depend on him and decides not to top himself. The End. And then you cry.'

'Still not sure we're living in the same universe, my

friend,' said the woman who'd just started a fiercely competitive chess game with a half-grown cat. 'What sort of counter offer do you have in mind?'

'A walk. Just to get some air. Doesn't necessarily have to be fresh.'

'Good thing too, this being the city,' she murmured. 'Chater Garden's not that far from you. There's greenery, topiary, a water feature or two… Ignore the concrete.'

'Sounds like I need a guide.'

'You really don't,' she said, smiling.

'But what if I want a guide?'

'Tell you what,' she said, feeling generous. 'What say I meet you at Chater Garden in half an hour? I'll be the one wearing the peacock feather in her hair.'

'One of these days I'll ask you why,' he murmured. 'I'll be the one in the Panama hat.'

Damon didn't know what had possessed him to seek out Ruby Maguire again today. Last night had been enough, more than enough to let him know that he should leave this one alone. Not for him a woman who could strip him bare. Never for him a woman who could access the secrets he kept in his soul.

Restlessness plagued him as he made his way to the park.

Tension rode him as he tried to figure out exactly what he would say to the woman who'd gifted him with something special last night. Maybe the words *whatever you gave to me, take it back* would be enough.

Just a walk in the park with a pretty woman on his arm and a burning desire to let her know that last night had been nothing more than a pleasant Christmas Eve diversion. That it didn't grant him any hold on her, or her on him. He wasn't sure he'd spelled that out last night.

He had a feeling he'd lost track of that particular notion around about the time he and Ruby had found themselves alone in the limo.

No regrets—he knew they'd covered that one.

But no promises? What exactly *had* he promised her last night that he shouldn't have? What had he given away?

Information? Of a certainty he'd revealed more than enough about his work, and he knew it, but he'd stopped, hadn't he? She *knew* his limits in that regard. She'd *accepted* them.

Had he revealed his total inexperience when it came to letting someone see him, really see him, for what he was? He probably had. Didn't mean he planned on doing it *again* in a hurry.

What else had he revealed in the back of that limo? A propensity for getting lost in passion? Well, if he had, Ruby had of a surety revealed the same. No crime there.

So why—as he watched her walk along the garden path towards him, in her pretty blue sundress with her tumbling curls pinned back with a peacock-feathered comb—did he feel so exposed?

Ruby Maguire's eyes were knowing as they met his. 'I figured as much,' she said wryly as she stopped before him. 'You're here to tell me that last night was a mistake. That I shouldn't expect a great deal from you. The word *nothing* comes to mind.'

'That about covers it,' he said gruffly.

'Well,' she said lightly, a vision of poise and loveliness and behind the pretty picture a brain that ran razor-sharp when it came to reading people. 'Seems to me you wasted your time in getting me here if that was the agenda, for it's nothing I don't already know. You overplayed the light-hearted, carefree Damon on the phone, by the way, if you want to know what really tipped me off. It just wasn't you. Still...' she looked skywards and smiled '...it's a nice day for a stroll and I wanted to get out of the apartment. You don't mind if I use you as a distraction, do you?'

Was yes even a *possible* answer after such a gracious and glossy dismissal of his concerns regarding her developing some kind of unwanted attachment to him? 'No.'

He tipped his hat and held out his arm, and he even managed a self-mocking smile as she slipped her hand in the crook of his arm, and without a word they began to stroll.

'You excel at making things easy for others, don't you, Ruby?' he offered at last. 'And somewhere in the process you get exactly what you want. It's very impressive.'

'It's a gift,' she said dulcetly.

'Or a weapon,' he countered dryly. 'Where'd you hone that razor-sharp mind of yours, Ruby?'

'Harvard.'

It figured. 'Where did *you* study?' she asked.

Damon hesitated, and Ruby sighed.

'Never mind,' she said. 'I forgot who I was talking to. Although may I point out that sticking entirely to the immediate present when conversing with *anyone* is a lot like talking to a brick. Nonetheless, I shall endeavour to oblige and make it easier for you to keep your secrets to yourself. See that building to the West, overlooking the park?' She waved a slender hand in its direction. 'That's Hong Kong's legislative council building. It's one of the reasons there are so many political demonstrations and marches here in the park. As for the park's history, did you know that these grounds once housed the most hallowed of colonial institutions, the Hong Kong Cricket Club?'

'MIT,' said Damon tightly, and stopped Ruby's fact-spouting dead. 'I studied mathematics and computer programming at MIT.'

The hand resting in the crook of his arm tightened, and Ruby came to a standstill. Damon turned to find her regarding him with a mixture of frustration and puzzlement.

'What?' he said. 'You asked, I answered. I was just…'

'Filtering,' she said wryly. Which he had been. 'Trust me, Damon. I know this game. My father never talked much beyond the moment either. You'd have liked him, by the way. He could have certainly shown you a trick or two about sliding graciously past a question you're not inclined to answer.'

'How would he have slid past that one?'

'Oh, I dare say he'd have started spouting rhetoric about the measurement of man,' said Ruby with a smile. 'From there you might have swung through a deeply philosophical discussion of the education system or if he gauged you differently perhaps he'd have offered you a champagne and piled on the flattery as he guessed which of the top twenty learning institutes in the world *you* graduated from.'

'Have you heard from him today?'

'Why do you ask?'

Damon shrugged and realised he didn't have any good answer other than Ruby drew him in, even when he didn't want to be drawn, and got to him when he didn't want to be got. 'Maybe it's because I know what it's like to wait for word that never comes.'

'He hasn't been in touch.'

And then she leaned into him, butting up against his arm with her body as if she craved connection, and he knew that feeling and that shoulder shove because he'd used it on Poppy as a child. Remember me, it had been shorthand for. The one who cost us our mother by dint of being born. The one who never quite managed to shake his feeling of isolation, even within the arms of family.

So he did what Poppy used to do, and put his arm around Ruby's shoulder and hugged her to his side and kept her there. He could do that much for her. He did it without thinking.

'I really hoped he'd call, you know?' she said finally, with her arm around his waist and their footsteps in sync as they followed the path before them. 'So that I'd know he was okay. That he was alive. That's the worst part of all of this mess. The not knowing *anything*.'

He should have realised that a woman of Ruby's ilk would have thought past the most obvious reason for her father's absence from her life. That she would have considered all sorts of explanations for her father's disappearance, few of them palatable. 'You think there's been foul play?'

'I don't know,' she murmured. 'My father had many faults, don't get me wrong. Branding him a hero's just… dumb. But I always thought he cared for me, and the way he left—without even the slightest goodbye or heads up…it doesn't make sense. It doesn't feel right.'

'Maybe he was protecting you. You know the terminology, Ruby. Accomplice. Accessory after the fact.'

'He was smart enough to avoid all that and still say goodbye.'

If he'd wanted to. But Damon didn't say that and Ruby didn't go there either.

'So what do you think *did* happen?' he asked quietly. 'You think he could have been trying to stop the theft?'

'If I thought that, I'd have to prepare for the possibility that he's dead. I don't want to prepare for that possibility, Damon.'

'It seems to me you already have.'

'No.' Ruby looked to the sky and the skyscrapers that crowded into it. 'I haven't. Not yet. Maybe not ever. Not as long as there's hope.'

Not a fine Christmas Day for Ruby Maguire at all. In behind the peacock feathers and the smiles, Ruby Maguire was hurting.

'You know what you need this afternoon?' he said, and pressed his lips to her hair for good measure. 'A strictly temporary, don't read anything into this, distraction. Lucky for you, I'm a past *Master* at distracting people. As every last one of my school reports will attest.'

'Why, Damon West.' She sounded less morose already. 'Was that freely volunteered information?'

'I think it was. But don't distract me while I'm busy trying to distract you. I hear there's a hell of a roller-coaster ride around here somewhere.'

'Yes, but in order to get *on* it one has to plan ahead.'

'Or we could go and play on the midlevel elevators, that's always fun.'

'Well, if you're a two-year-old...'

'Golf!' he said, inspired.

'Spare me.'

'Shopping?'

Ruby Maguire rewarded him with a smile. 'I'm vastly impressed by your sacrifice, but no. Nothing much is open.'

'Swimming?'

'Maybe later.'

'Mah-jong?'

'But we'd need a third player.'

'Poppy'll play if we ask her. She might even know how.'

'Meaning you've never played?' asked Ruby delicately.

'No, but how hard could it be?'

'I like your optimism.' Her smile had widened. Her eyes held a hint of mischief. 'I suppose I could teach you the basics and then if Poppy wanted to join us she'd be most welcome. Were you to, say, enhance the speed of your learning experience by putting your money where your optimism is I would indeed be most delightfully distracted.'

'You have all the essentials?'

The peacock feather bobbed up and down vigorously as she nodded. 'Everything but your blank cheque.'

Ruby's apartment held its own when it came to luxury and location. Size wise, it only had two bedrooms, one of which she used as an office, but the lounge and dining area was plenty large enough for a crowd, and more than large enough for a fleecing.

'There's a kitten around here somewhere,' she said as she put her handbag on the side table and picked up the remote and switched the music on and drew the curtains back. Not Christmas tunes, heaven forbid, but rather a brother and sister duo whose music played light and ethereal and wormed its way into the soul one wisp at a time.

'You mean this kitten?' Ruby turned and there was the kitten, creeping out from behind the couch and venturing closer to Damon than he'd ever ventured to her without serious coaxing.

'That's him, and you're doing well. He's the wary type. I like to think he'll turn out to be a sweet and loving companion once we move past the outright mistrust stage but that's just pure and hopeful speculation.'

'Have you considered getting a dog?' asked Damon dryly as the little cat took cover behind the leg of the coffee table.

But Ruby wasn't quite mad enough to bring a dog to this city of sky rises and crowded concrete living. 'Not for here,' she said as she foraged in the fridge for the Christmas nibbles she'd stocked up on just in case, say, an army decided to drop in unexpectedly. 'Maybe if I lived on a ranch, or a tropical island. Australia…'

'Ever *been* to Australia?'

'Well, no. But I'm sure a dog could be very happy there. Its owner too.'

'Let me know if you ever want to try it some time,' he murmured. 'I have a beach house on the East Coast that I never use. You could stay there. No resident dog though.'

'Damon West, I stand corrected. You're not a homeless person after all.'

He smiled at that. 'Does it make you think better of me?'

'No, but your offer does. It's very generous. Also somewhat surprising. What if I were to discover some of those well-kept secrets of yours while I was there?'

'Well, you could try,' he said with supreme confidence as she set a jug of water and frosty glasses on the breakfast bar beside the food. 'We could have a little wager on it.'

'That's the spirit,' she said encouragingly and offered him a candied ginger. 'May I get you a drink? Inhibition-loosening beverage of your choice?'

'And if you miss out on a suitable job in Geneva you can always try the casinos in Monte Carlo,' he offered dryly. 'They'd have you in a heartbeat.'

'I'll keep that in mind,' she murmured, and he smiled his lazy smile and popped a candy in his mouth.

He reached for the hat on his head and set it on the breakfast stool next to him, making himself at home in her space, working his charm because she'd asked him to. Because she'd done enough soul-searching for today, and they could hammer out the details of their relationship another time, or just let it flow, considering that they both appeared to be on the same page when it came to knowing nothing permanent would come of it.

Didn't mean she couldn't appreciate and enjoy the gifts that he brought to her table today. The simple gift of being there. The rogue's gifts of distraction and entertainment. His hug for her earlier, the gift of human touch. His understanding of her predicament when it came to her father. He had family he hadn't heard from recently too.

'Have you heard from your brother?' One last serious question before she allowed herself to be seriously distracted.

'No.'

'Are you worried about him?'

'Lena is. I'm a little more inclined to give him some leeway. Jared's big on guilt at the moment because Lena nearly died under his command. Lena wants him home so she can tell him to get over it. My guess is that Jared's gone after the people who hurt her and that he'll be back when he can deliver up their heads on a plate and not before.'

'Oh.' What to say to that? 'It sounds…plausible.' If one discounted the fact that, out head-hunting or not, surely brother Jared would have found an opportunity to call home by now.

'I know how it sounds, Ruby. But we're used to not hearing from Jared for long stretches at a time. I'm not that worried about him. Yet.'

'Good,' she said sincerely. 'Here's to your brother getting his revenge and finding his way home.'

'You're not going to say he should leave it to the legal system?'

'Justice takes many forms, my friend. The legal system delivers but one of them.'

'They teach you that in law school?'

'No, that one comes with age and experience.'

'Imagine how cynical you'll be by the time you're sixty.'

'I know,' she said. 'Frightening. I have a feeling you're going to like mah-jong. It's a game of great subtlety. The wind blows and the probabilities turn. Dragons roar and the path ahead changes. Flexibility is the key. I'll show you the play, which you'll pick up fast, and I'll let you figure out the mathematical probabilities for yourself. Wouldn't want that fancy maths degree of yours to go to waste.'

'You're too kind.'

'I know.' She opened the case and watched Damon's gaze sharpen upon the tiles as most everyone's did when they first viewed the set. Pewter-backed jade, each piece exquisitely carved and painted and then polished to high gloss—each tile so perfectly matched to the next that there could be no telling them apart once they were face down.

'It's said this set once belonged to the emperor's favourite concubine and that she won many a concession from her lover when the tiles were played. I hope you don't mind if we play on a velvet cloth,' she murmured dulcetly. 'It's a very sensual experience. And of course it protects the pieces.'

Damon made no reply, just started in on his shirt buttons and then peeled it off and handed it to her. 'This being the shirt off my back,' he said. 'Take it. It'll save time.'

'It's also rumoured that a lot of games between the emperor and his concubine remained unfinished.' Ruby took the shirt from him and steeled herself not to ogle his very fine form. 'Now I know why.'

'Happy to do as much illuminating as you want on that score, Ruby. He was probably trying to distract her.'

'Well, I'm sure she appreciated his efforts,' she murmured. 'What a giver.'

Damon smiled, slow and lazy, and Ruby shivered, and not with apprehension. Something about this man called to her and it wasn't just his beautiful body and it certainly wasn't his zealously guarded mind. Maybe it was the yearning she sensed in his soul.

'C'mere,' he said, and Ruby went and gave herself over to him willingly, to the taste of him and the responsiveness of her skin beneath his touch. A fleeting kiss and then another as he teased her lips with his and made the ache inside her grow.

'Distracted yet?' he murmured.

'Very.'

She found places for her hands on his chest. A puckered nipple beneath one palm and the ridges of his stomach beneath another. 'Last night,' she whispered, 'was so…so…'

'Don't say disappointing.'

'Unexpected.' As he slid her hair comb from her hair and set his lips to the skin behind her ear. 'And unbelievably hot. I've been trying to figure out the why of it all morning.'

'I'm blaming it on the limo,' he whispered, threading his fingers through her hair and drawing her into an open-mouthed kiss that as far as Ruby was concerned destroyed his limo argument outright. 'All that forced intimacy.'

'I'm thinking of blaming it on Santa,' she offered, and closed her eyes the better to concentrate on the fire in his touch.

'Not exactly a reasoned argument.'

Ruby countered by sliding her hand down until she found the iron-hard length of him, deeply satisfied when he groaned and surged against her hand and then in one swift movement picked her up and planted her on the table, her legs wide as he stepped in between them and showed her exactly where he wanted that shaft to be. 'Better than yours, though. Where's the limo now?'

'What limo?' he muttered and his eyes were dark with desire. 'Where's your bed?'

'Down the hall, first door on the right.'

By the time they got there Ruby's clothes were gone and so were his, two of the hallway pictures were askew and the walls had received a battering.

He gave himself so freely to pleasure, and Ruby did too, until they were both bathed in touch and taste and the heady scent of arousal, and then he rolled until she sat astride him and he positioned her for his entry and made it slow and glorious.

Ruby closed her eyes and wrapped her hands around his forearms while he sat up and worked his clever lips and tongue over her neck and throat. Piling distraction upon distraction and lacing it with an abandon she couldn't resist.

There were no rules with this man. She wanted him

at her breast, and he took it with a groan and paid attention and made her scream. He kissed his way down her body after that, and he turned her on her back and took her hands and wrapped her fingers around the wrought-iron bed bars above her head and told her to keep them there and then proceeded to string kisses across her stomach and her hip, her thigh and finally her core, and he knew what he was doing, heaven help her he did, and she entreated him and cursed him in the same breath as he took her to a land far, far away.

There'd been a magical quality to last night's lovemaking that had taken Ruby unawares and turned the night golden, and today was no different.

He made her feel loved, and he made her feel beautiful as he let her ride out her climax and then entered her as if he couldn't wait a moment longer.

'Now you can touch me,' he whispered, and touch him she did, only she could never quite get enough, and her need built again, he made damn sure of that.

Need over reason, for how could reason explain this?

'Let go, Damon, just let go now. I'll come with you, I swear I will.'

And it was as if her words released the leash he'd kept on himself and stripped away every barrier. He shuddered hard and clung to her as he spilled himself deep inside her, and Ruby flew with him this time, not even half a heartbeat behind as together they found oblivion.

Just as she'd promised.

'The things you do to me,' he murmured as they lay on the bed, both of them on their backs, their bodies spent and separate but the connection between them running stronger than ever. He lifted his arm from his elbow down, made a fist and then stretched his fingers wide, and Ruby raised her hand to his and he threaded his fingers through hers. 'The concessions you wring from me.'

'I'd hardly call a thimbleful of honesty between lovers a concession,' she murmured lazily. 'Although maybe in your case I should. Maybe you should favour me with another example of your concessions, just so I can identify them in future.'

'Give me five minutes and I'll get right onto it.' He shot her a lazy, satisfied smile. 'Maybe ten.'

'Give me a memory from your childhood, something you don't usually reveal, and I'll give you anything you want.'

'Big promises, Empress.'

'Chances are I'll never have to deliver, Concession Boy.'

He closed his eyes. He shut her out. 'My mother died giving birth to me,' he said quietly. 'Not something I tell the world.'

Careful where your wishes take you, Ruby, she thought grimly, but it was too late to turn back now. 'That's understandable.'

Damon said nothing.

'Did your family hold it against you?'

'No,' he said. 'Never.'

Ruby let go of Damon's hand, the better to prop herself up on one elbow and look at him. But she slid her other hand in his the minute she could and he didn't pull away. 'I'm glad to hear it,' she said simply.

'Didn't stop me from spending most of my teens try-ing to push them away.'

'And then you got over yourself?' she asked hope-fully, and he smiled wryly and brought her hand to his chest.

'Let's just say I finally figured out how much I needed them. And how much they needed me to come good. To make their loss worthwhile. To make it mean something.'

'Or, they could've just been waiting for you to stop beating yourself up over something you had no control over so that you could finally see how much they loved you. That'd work too. As an argument for persistence in the face of your rebellion.'

'The lawyer speaks.'

'Well, if reasoned argument isn't working for you, I dare say I could always try kissing you better. Provided of course that you tell me where it hurts.'

'My shoulder,' he murmured, his eyes dark and guarded, and she kissed his shoulder and he took a shuddering breath.

'My chest,' he said next and she kissed him above his heart and then she took his nipple in her mouth and Damon loosened his hold on her hand and the next thing she knew his hand was in her hair, the better to hold her against him.

'My side.' Little more than a rumble, but she heard him and she kissed him there, as he started to stiffen against her once more, ten minutes to resurrection be damned.

'Where else?' she whispered.

'You know where.'

'Say it.'

But he didn't say a word.

'Why, Damon West,' she said with a grin and slid her mouth another inch or two down his stupendous body. 'I do believe you're repressed. Who knew?'

'I am not repr—' he began warningly, and then she licked and made a meal out of him and he sucked in his breath and shut the hell up.

'Something on your mind?' she murmured long moments later. 'Because you'd tell me if there was, right?'

'Right,' he rasped.

'Liar.' She found the base of him and kissed him there and set her hand to him and he caught her hair up in his hands and strained within her grasp. 'This, by the way, is *my* concession to you and I do hope you like it. Feel free to distract me whenever you've had enough.' Damon groaned. Ruby licked.

'Is my hand too tight?' She slid it slowly up and down the generous length of him. 'Mouth too warm?' She slid that up and down the length of him too and interpreted his guttural groan as a no. 'Because you'd tell me, right?'

'Right.'

He let her pleasure him, for a time. And then he lifted her into his arms and slid inside her and Ruby could have cried at how right it felt to make love with this particular man, lose herself in him even.

But she didn't cry and she didn't say a word about how easily he could shatter her defences. Nor did she mention the decidedly inconvenient and somewhat frightening fact that she'd never felt this way with any-one before.

Ruby Maguire knew how to keep secrets too.

CHAPTER SIX

THE aftermath of love-making wasn't always easy, conceded Damon. There could be awkwardness and boundaries to re-establish. Control to find. Leave to be taken, provided clothes could be found. So far, Damon had managed to find his clothes. Ruby hadn't even managed that, but then, she didn't have family waiting and wondering where the hell she was.

'What time is it?' she said.

'Four.'

'That late?' She sat up abruptly, every inch the dishevelled wanton, and the corners of Damon's mouth kicked in response.

'I'm taking that as a compliment.'

'And so you should.' Ruby slipped from the bed and found her dress, no awkwardness in her whatsoever and it helped ease his. 'Your powers of distraction are truly—' Ruby laid a hand over her heart '—*truly* stupendous.'

Damon smiled at her words and turned away and headed for the en-suite. There'd been a hell of a lot more than distraction going on here this afternoon, but if Ruby wasn't inclined to point it out then he certainly wasn't going to. Ruby—it seemed—had bypassed awkwardness and moved straight to the setting of boundaries. Which was fine by him.

No promises and no regrets. They could do this. And then Ruby came into the bathroom with her dress on and leaned back against the bench as he splashed his face with water and took the hand towel she offered him.

'I need to get going soon,' he said, and wondered at his sudden reluctance to move.

'Want a lift?' And when he studied the towel instead of answering, 'I can drop you at the door?' He moved away from the basin and Ruby took his place, took one look in the mirror and gasped and then grabbed for her hairbrush. 'Boy, am I dropping you at the door.'

'You look fine.' He took the brush from her and stepped in behind her, setting brush to hair. His gaze met Ruby's in the mirror and it hit him like a train that he wanted this picture in his life. Wanted it with an intensity he usually reserved for his work. 'And you're welcome to come in.'

'No. Thank you, but no. If you're planning on attending your father's Boxing Day luncheon I'll see you tomorrow. If you're not…'

'I'll be there,' he murmured and handed her back her brush. 'I'll be at my father's until the thirtieth.'

'More information?' she purred. 'Why, Damon. You spoil me.'

'No, I don't.' But he wanted to.

'Anyway…' she said with a shrug that reminded him of the shrugs of his youth. The ones designed to make people think he wasn't hurting. 'Time to get you home.'

She drove him to his father's door. And then she smiled and blew him a kiss and drove away.

* * *

Russell West's inaugural Boxing Day luncheon had been Ruby's idea. An informal drop-in for business associates and friends, it started at midday and would go on until late as guests cycled through, staying for as long or as short a time as they wanted. The caterers were the best in the business and came complete with service manager and wait staff, which left Ruby very little to do but stay out of the way unless issues arose.

Instigator she might have been but host she was not. She left that to Russell and his family and could not fault any of them. Both Poppy and Lena were wearing the clothes she'd chosen for them. Both looked stunning—even if she did say so herself.

Ruby wore a simple ivory skirt and jacket with a violet camisole beneath. No lace. No frou-frou at all except for a tiny crystal-embedded hair clip to hold her hair up and out of her face. Her father's reputation preceded her these days, but she did her best to be unobtrusive in this type of company so that her presence would not reflect poorly on Russell.

No need for people to know how Russell had come by his recent social savvy. All they needed to know was that a new social circle had opened up and that it glowed with opportunity when it came to matching investors with developers, visionaries with the more practically minded, movers and shakers with those who could oil their way.

Damn right no one paid her any attention—everyone was too busy doing what they did best.

Ruby allowed herself a tiny smile. At least two major business deals would get stitched up here today. Maybe three. Not bad for a former corporate lawyer turned social PA.

'Ruby? Is that you?'

Ruby looked up at the sound of her name, her smile turning genuine as she recognised the speaker. 'Juliet! How are you? It's been too long. And you are *still* the most beautiful woman I've ever seen. I want your secret.'

'Flatterer,' said the other woman warmly as they exchanged kisses. 'Your father taught you well.'

'So true.' Ruby stood back and caught the other woman's hand. 'I heard you'd remarried. Renauld Lang, yes?'

'Yes.' Juliet's face softened. 'He's a good man, Ruby. A kind man. I got lucky.'

'You deserved to,' murmured Ruby gently. Juliet had been Ruby's father's lover once and had made the fatal mistake of getting serious about him, and befriending Ruby, and trying, bless Juliet's gentle heart, to make a place for herself in Harry Maguire's life.

It hadn't ended well.

'I know what they're saying about your father, Ruby,' said Juliet gently. 'And for what it's worth I don't believe a word of it. Harry was restless, and ruthless, and frustratingly enigmatic more often than not. But he wasn't a thief and he would *never* have walked away from you. You know that, don't you?'

'Sometimes I know it,' said Ruby with a wry smile. 'It means a lot to hear you say it.'

'Any time,' said the other woman gently.

'Ladies,' said a deeply delicious voice with just the right amount of wickedness in it. 'I'm doing the rounds on behalf of my father. May I interest either of you in a drink?'

Ruby looked up and her smile grew even wryer as she took in the elegance that was Damon all suited up and primed to behave. 'Juliet Lang, Damon West,' said Ruby. 'Juliet and I are old acquaintances. Damon and I are new acquaintances. Juliet, will you have a champagne?'

'Of course,' said the older woman.

'What about you, Ruby?' asked Damon.

'Thanks, but no. I'm working. I have a glass of water around here somewhere.'

Damon nodded and moved away and Ruby watched him go. She'd been trying not to watch him for the best part of the afternoon. The way he mingled easily and endured his father's pride in him with wry good humour. The way he drew daughters, wives and grandmothers to him like locusts to a plague.

Charmer, no question.

Be whatever someone wanted him to be.

'Impressive,' murmured Juliet.

'Very. But strictly short term.'

'Heartbreaker,' said Juliet warningly.

'Only if you let him be.'

Ruby smiled and found her glass, caught his gaze and sent him a silent and appreciative toast.

'Don't bait the man, Ruby. Didn't your father ever tell you not to play with fire?'

'He did,' said Ruby. 'But it's so much fun.'

She laughed with Juliet for a while and met her lovely husband, and then it was time to slip away and do the rounds of the powder rooms to make sure they were tidy and well stocked. Three bathrooms available to guests. Two off the atrium and living areas and another at the end of the hallway, past the guest bedrooms.

Ruby's shoes clickety-clacked as she made her way back down the hallway towards the mingling throng of powerful people, and then her shoes stopped their noise-making midstride as a strong arm snaked out from a bedroom doorway and drew her inside onto carpeted floor. The bedroom door closed firmly behind her, and then Damon backed her against it and set his hands either side of her head and his lips to the curve of her neck.

'Damon, I'm working,' she whispered, even as her hands went to his waist and she tilted her head to allow him better access. 'What are we? Twelve?'

'I prefer to think of it as innovative,' he murmured silkily and then set his hungry mouth to hers, at which point all talking ceased for quite a while. More kisses followed. Delicate open-mouthed explorations that fed desire. Deep and drugging declarations of desire gone mad. Whatever this was, Ruby could no longer control it, and as for Damon…

'God, Ruby.'

He seemed bent on encouraging the insanity.

And then the doorknob turned and the door at her back began to open and Damon slammed it shut with the palm of his hand. Ruby stilled and stared at Damon, the fear of discovery heady when mixed with desire.

Who? she mouthed silently and Damon just shook his head and raised an eyebrow, but he didn't open the door and for that she was truly grateful.

The doorknob turned again and this time Damon frowned. 'Who is it?' he said.

'Lena.'

Damon grimaced, and his gaze cut from Ruby's face to the en-suite doorway.

Silently, Ruby ducked beneath his arm and made her way to the en-suite and carefully shut the door behind her. Damon's cue now, to open the door to Lena and guide her elsewhere so that Ruby could make her escape.

She heard the door open and Damon's guarded, 'What is it?' and Lena's exasperated, 'For heaven's sake, Damon. Let me in. What is *wrong* with you?'

'I was just coming back *out*,' said Damon, and in the relative safety of the bathroom Ruby nodded her agreement.

'Wait,' said Lena. 'I need to talk to you. Privately.'

Not good. Definitely not good.

'Now,' said Lena firmly, and, cursing silently, Ruby closed her eyes and leaned back against the wall to wait.

'Lena, not now. This really isn't a good time.'

But Lena wasn't listening and Damon stood back and let his sister into the room. Better to get it over with then, whatever it was, for Lena had that look on her face. The one that promised no mercy whatsoever for whoever had been stupid enough to irritate her in the first place to the point of explosion.

'Why didn't you tell me you had news on Jared's whereabouts?'

'What?' he said warily.

'Last night you told me you hadn't found a thing. Today Poppy tells me that you've already hacked into the ASIS database and found Jared's personnel record and pulled a coded file from the system that you now need Poppy to decode.'

'Lena, please,' he said urgently and pressed his fingers to her lips, something he should have done the moment she'd stepped in the room, only he'd still been dazed from Ruby's kisses and he hadn't even seen it coming. 'Not now.'

But she wrenched his hand away, eyes flashing. 'Why not? Am I too fragile to know the truth all of a sudden? Is that it?'

'Lena—'

'You *lied* to me. You sat there the other day and you lied to my face.'

'No, I told you I didn't have any information on Jared's whereabouts. I still don't.'

'Don't you *dare* pull that half-truth crap on me. Hacking might be your business, and secrecy your way of life, but I am your *sister* and this is Jared we're talking about. How could you? How could you shut me out? Has it not occurred to you that I might be able to help? That I might know ASIS operational systems and codes better than you?'

'Lena. Not. Now,' he said through gritted teeth.

'*Why* not now?'

And then the en-suite door opened and Ruby stood there pale but composed, and looking anywhere but at him.

'Probably because he doesn't want anyone overhearing your conversation,' she said quietly. 'So if you'll excuse me, I'm just going to…leave. Thanks, Damon, for the, ah, use of your bathroom.'

Smiling brightly, Ruby executed a hasty exit and shut the door firmly behind her.

'Oh, *hell*,' said Lena and stared at him in dismay. 'Damon, I'm so sorry—'

But Damon was already halfway out of the door.

He found her directing the wait staff with the precision of a conquering general. He stood back and watched, and let her do her thing and manoeuvre guests and charm her father. She hadn't fled, she had a job to do, and it suited Damon to stand and watch her do it while he planned how best to deal with a situation he'd never encountered before.

He went back to his room, with a bleak-eyed glare for Lena, who passed him in the hallway, where he filled his backpack with the things he would need and then returned to the main room and simply walked up to her in the kitchen, took her hand and headed for the door and to hell with what people thought. His father would get over it. His father's business friends and associates could think what they liked, and as for Ruby...

If she objected to his high-handedness she made no mention of it as she collected her work satchel from the cloak cupboard and strode through the apartment door he'd opened for her, with her hand still firmly ensconced in his.

Perhaps she was as glad to see the back end of the party as he was. Perhaps she had something to say. Time would tell, because she sure as hell wasn't saying anything now.

Such a fascinating face—the one she presented to him as they stepped into the lift and turned around to

face the closing doors. Not classically beautiful—no
Grace Kelly here—but those eyes could drown a man
and her lips were the work of a master. A lovely, lively
face, and if a man preferred it to classical perfection,
well, that was his preference.

If a man wanted to walk blindfold off a cliff and en-
trust her with his darkest secrets, well…that was his
business too.

They rode the lift in silence, all the way down to the
car park and only when they were heading for her car
did she finally choose to speak.

'So… I don't know much about hacking but I do
know that the term *hacker* can have multiple meanings,'
she began quietly. Careful words from a lawyer's mind.
Ruby Maguire was thinking things through. 'What kind
of hacker are you? Or perhaps the more appropriate
question would be, to what *end* do you hack?'

'You cross-examining me, Ruby?'

'You planning on answering the question, Damon?'

Impasse.

'Because, please correct me if I'm wrong, but it
sounded to me as if you hack to acquire information.
Like your brother's whereabouts, for example.'

'That one's more of an unofficial side project de-
tour…thing. Tiny. Really.'

'Right,' she drawled cuttingly. 'So the rest of your
work relates to the *official* collection of restricted information. How very reassuring.'

'Shades of grey, Ruby,' he murmured and Ruby shot
him a filthy glare.

'So you're a spy. An information thief, all jacked
in, new millennium style.' And when he said nothing,

'God, Damon. Have you *any* idea how many ethical buttons this pushes for me? There *are* other ways of getting information. Legal ways.'

'Like, for example, you asking the FBI to share whatever information they have on your father? How's that working out for you, Ruby?'

'Shut up.'

'Second oldest profession, or so they say. It's not as if I'm breaking new ground here. Just newer ways of doing it. I work towards maintaining peaceful power balances between nations. How is that wrong?'

Ruby's steps had quickened, her chest rising and falling rapidly. Damon walked too, silence clearly the best option for now. How the hell had he got *into* this mess?

Headbands were the devil's work, he decided grimly. The next time he saw one he'd know to run.

'I knew you had secrets,' she said and fumbled through her satchel for her car keys. 'I chose to spend time with you anyway. But this... I've got to hand it to you, Damon. Even for me this is a whole new level of secrets and lies. I *knew* I should have stayed away from you,' she muttered. 'Why the *hell* didn't I?'

He had no answer for her there. 'You can't tell anyone, Ruby.'

'Yes, I gathered that,' she said, and raised a shaking hand to her head. 'Who else knows?'

'My immediate family. My handler. Now you. Six people in ten years.' It wasn't a bad effort. He didn't think it *too* bad a record.

'God.' She looked worried and so she should be. 'I won't tell anyone, Damon. You have my word.'

'And in an ideal world, your word would be enough,'

he said quietly, but this wasn't an ideal world. He needed to secure her silence and her loyalty. Bind her to him now, with whatever he had in hand.

'What if I said I could help you find your father?'

'*What?*'

'That's what you want, isn't it?'

'Yes, but...'

She didn't, or couldn't, finish her sentence. Typical lawyer. Always a But.

'I'm offering to contract out to you,' he continued. 'In return for your silence. You get news of your father. I acquire a hold on you I currently don't have. Everyone wins.'

'That's blackmail.'

'It's necessary,' he cut back hard. 'And at the end of the day you get to walk away, I get the peace of mind I need to let you walk away and the people I work for get to remain none the wiser as to what you know. That's worth something, Ruby. More than you know.'

'Well, aren't you chivalrous,' she murmured, and favoured him with a tight-lipped smile.

'I try.'

This discussion wasn't exactly going according to plan, decided Damon grimly. But then, nothing involving Ruby ever did.

'I'm trying to *protect* you,' he said curtly, and maybe Ruby heard the frustration in him for she eyed him uncertainly before looking to the car-park walls for answers, only there were none to be had there. He'd already looked.

'Or I could let my superiors know I've broken cover with you and let them deal with the fallout. They won't

harm you, they'll recruit you. Like it or not, you won't
have a choice. That's the value they place on the work
I do for them, Ruby. The cost of maintaining my cover.
And the reason I never wanted you to know any of this
in the first place.'

'I knew you were trouble,' she said again. 'I knew.'

Again, Damon said nothing. It wasn't as if she were
telling him anything new.

'How would you do it?' she said after a time. 'My
father could be anywhere. How would you set about
finding him? Where would you even start?'

'I'd access files various authorities have on him and
get you to read them. See if what they have to say fits
with what you remember. See if it throws up any ideas.
And then we'll continue from there.'

'Couldn't you just…send me a report?'

'Sorry, Ruby. You don't get to stay clean while I get
dirty for you. I want you with me.'

'And equally culpable.'

Damon shrugged. The short answer being yes.

She looked ready to weep but she tilted her chin and
squared her shoulders. 'When do you need my answer
on this?'

'Now.'

'And when would we do it?'

He gentled his tone and hoped for her sake she could
handle this. 'Just as soon as we get you back to your
apartment and get into different clothes.'

'What kind of clothes?' Ruby was willing to be distracted by the little things. It was a start.

'The kind that don't stand out.'

CHAPTER SEVEN

IF RUBY could press a rewind button she would.

This day would disappear for starters.

Russell's society luncheon would go.

She wouldn't go so far as to wipe Damon from memory completely but there were definitely things she would have done differently when it came to dealing with him.

Such as not push him for personal information he so clearly hadn't wanted to give.

And not allow herself to become so enamoured of the physical side of their relationship that she lost all sense of self-preservation.

Fooling around with Damon in his bedroom, with a party in full swing not six yards away. What kind of idiot behaviour was that?

She'd thought she could play with Damon without consequence. Use him, as it were. She really had thought she could be intimate with him and come away unscathed.

Wrong.

'First a father who may or may not be guilty of the biggest heist in banking history, and now a computer hacker for a lover,' she murmured, and a small cat

peeked out from beneath her bed and regarded her solemnly. 'I'm really not having a good run. And what the
hell kind of clothes does a person wear when commit-
ting a hacking offence?'

Damon had clothes in his backpack, or so he said.
He'd retired to Ruby's bathroom to get changed.

Ruby tossed her jacket on the bed and began to rifle
through her wardrobe. Jeans, they'd do. A black T-shirt
she usually wore when cleaning things. Flat shoes...
apart from the ones she wore around the apartment,
and they were little more than slippers, flat shoes really weren't in her vocabulary. Almost-flat shoes, by
way of a pair of black patent leather pumps with black
and white spotted bows across the front of them, would
have to do.

She put her hair up in a ponytail, left it ornament-free
and returned to the lounge room in search of Damon,
the man with the vagabond lifestyle, the secrets she
didn't want to know, and a moral fluidity she couldn't
even begin to comprehend.

Don't judge.

Why did she always have to judge?

Damon had his Christmas jeans on and a grey T-shirt
and the battered black backpack slung across his shoulder now looked half-empty. She'd never seen him looking quite so downmarket before. Or so dangerous.

'Where are we going?' she asked tentatively.

'Out for some fast food.' He looked her over, frowned
when he got to her shoes. 'Lose the shoes, Ruby. Or at
least lose the bows.'

Fortunately for him, the bows came off without a
great deal of persuasion and would go on again under

the influence of superglue. 'Do I have to *eat* the fast food?' she said.

'It's tastier than it looks.'

'Only if you have the palate of a two-year-old.'

He smiled at that and some of the tension between them dissipated. 'It's my show, Ruby,' he said softly. 'Let's go.'

'Wait!' she said hastily. 'You don't want to talk about it first? Run me through what it is we'll be doing?'

'I'll talk you through it as we're doing it,' he offered calmly.

Ruby opened her mouth to protest, took one look at him, and shut it again without saying a word.

They walked from her apartment to the nearest train station. Just another young couple getting from one place to the next, foreigners but not strangers to Hong Kong or the mass transit railway service it provided.

Comfortable, as they found two free seats and Damon slung his backpack between his feet and laced her hand in his and smiled, before turning to look out of the train window into subway darkness, his thoughts his own.

'I should have bought a book,' she said lightly, and he fished his phone out of his pack and handed it to her.

'Take your pick.' And she took it because she was curious and scrolled though his offerings.

'No romance,' she said after a time and handed the phone back to him and earned herself a very level gaze. 'You said you'd explain what we were doing along the way. Why are we going to Kowloon?'

'To find an internet access point. One that tracks back to a public place.'

'Like a fast-food outlet?'

'Often they have internet access. Not that it'll do us any good. Too much surveillance. Not enough privacy.'

'So why are we doing the fast food thing at all?'

'I just like their coffee.'

He was deliberately messing with her head and from the glint in his eye he knew it.

'Once we get to Kowloon, we're looking for a combination of things within a short distance of each other,' he said quietly. 'A luxury hotel. A less than savoury hotel. And caffeine.'

'And then what?'

'And then we go to work.'

He found what he was looking for within five minutes of exiting the train station. Coffee stop at the fast-food place first, while Damon fiddled with his phone and largely ignored her. Normal behaviour for this part of the world, Ruby noted. Around here, mobile phones and miniature computers ruled supreme.

'All set?' he said, in less time than it took her to take two cautious sips of her surprisingly decent coffee. 'Bring it with you,' he said of her coffee. 'We're going to need a room.'

Not a room at the five-star hotel, however. No, Damon escorted her to a high rise nearby that boasted a bar on the ground floor, a hotel on the next, and several different categories of businesses after that, a brothel being one of them, given the nature of the girls lounging idly in the bar.

'One room, one night, a window facing the street, no company, no room service and no questions,' murmured Damon and handed a wad of Hong Kong dollars to the bruiser manning the reception desk.

'You got it,' said the bruiser and gave Damon a hotel swipe card and nodded towards the stairs.

'And another innkeepers' law bites the dust,' she murmured as they started up the stairs. Damon glanced at her, his gaze faintly mocking.

'Time to put the lawyer away, Ruby.'

'You don't say,' she countered grimly and stepped over a pile of what looked like discarded clothing on the stairs. 'Please tell me we're not staying here the night.'

'We're not staying here the night.'

Good news, because room 203 was charmless, airless and decidedly unclean. Ruby stood in the centre of the room sipping her suddenly mighty fine coffee and watched as Damon slung his backpack off his shoulder and withdrew a small laptop from within it. He set it on the bedside table beside the window and set its innards whirring.

'Pull up a chair,' he said, but Ruby didn't feel like sitting.

'Mind if I pace instead?'

'No pacing allowed,' he said. 'Sit.'

So she pulled up a chair and sat and stared at the computer screen, her heart beating too fast for comfort, and her eyes noticing the speed with which Damon's big hands flew over the keyboard. Logging into the internet somehow, without logging in.

'How do you know where to—? Oh, boy,' she whispered as all of a sudden they were somewhere within FBI-land and screen after screen of information was opening up in new windows, with Damon chasing them down, one by one, and entering string after string of code.

'Easy, Ruby,' he whispered, his eyes on the screen in front of him, his focus absolute. 'Relax.'

She wanted to ask him what he was doing and how he was doing it but she didn't have the breath for it.

'There's a rhythm to hacking, to navigating the information flow and pitting your wits against a security system built by another,' he said softly. 'For some, reaching their destination without detection is thrill enough. Others, they only want to destroy. For some of us, the destination is just a portal to a bigger game and it's a game based on power and knowledge and balance on the grandest of scales. That's my game, and it's more dangerous than you know. I need your silence on the issue, Ruby.'

'Believe me, you have it.'

'Not yet I don't.'

A blur of information. So fast; all of it too fast for comprehension. A download option.

Damon's hands falling away from the computer keys.

Ruby's breath coming rapid and strained, adrenalin coursing fiercely through her body as she stared at the little arrow on the screen that Damon had placed atop the download link.

'Your turn.'

Damon's voice low and husky as he transferred that intense focus to her face.

'It's the FBI's file on your father.'

Time slowed down to crawling as Ruby stared first at Damon and then at the screen. 'I, ah—I'm not—sure. Oh, *hell*,' she whispered, because she wanted that information and Damon had made it so easy for her to just reach out and take it.

'Or we leave the information where it is, I tell my handler I've blown my cover with you and we see how that unfolds.'

'No.' Not with her father's file sitting there just begging to be taken. 'My father's whereabouts in return for my silence. I get it, Damon. And I agree to your terms.' Her hand moved. The download began. Her choice, and she wore that knowledge like a stain.

'Guess I'm not as principled as I thought,' she said faintly.

'Who is?' muttered Damon, his focus back on the screen.

The file took an agonisingly slow ten seconds to download, and then Damon was back at the keyboard, fingers flying.

'You're getting out of the FBI pages now, right?' she said.

'Right.'

And straight into the British intelligence system, and Ruby's stomach lurched and her pulse rate soared all over again. 'Hell of a ride,' she said but he was gone again, skimming through supposedly secure cyberspace with an ease that made her gasp.

Another download link, but no agony of hesitation this time for Ruby. They were done and gone, with a swiftness she found hard to comprehend. All the way out this time. Two files stored on a USB the size of a thumbnail. Laptop off and opened up with a tiny screwdriver. One of the motherboard components replaced.

Fifteen minutes from start to finish, and they were

walking back down those shabby hotel stairs and hand-
ing the door card over to Reception.

'Any decent cheap *yum cha* restaurants around here?'
he asked the man, and got directions and nodded, while
Ruby sweated and smiled and tried to resist the urge to
flee.

'Please tell me we're not going back there,' she said
when they were two shopfronts away and Ruby was
walking faster than she'd ever walked before, every
nerve ending buzzing and every neon sign a thousand
times brighter than it had been fifteen minutes ago. She
ran her hands up and down her arms, mildly surprised
she didn't give off sparks. 'We're not, right?'

'Right.'

Damon's pace had quickened too. Ruby was practically skipping. 'So...where *are* we going?'

'Yum cha?'

'Are you serious?' He couldn't possibly be serious.
He was.

'Not *yum cha*,' she said. 'I wouldn't be able to sit
still. I'm feeling...'

'Wired.'

'Exactly.'

'It'll pass.'

'Yes, but *when*?'

'Soon,' he said with a kick to his mouth that warned
her she was amusing him.

'Look!' She pointed to a shopfront across the road.
'Chinese massage. They're very relaxing. We could
have one of those.'

'It's a brothel, Ruby.'

'Oh.' Ruby took a closer look. 'Brothel. Good pick-up. Maybe I just need to go back to the apartment and go for a swim. Soothing. Tactile. Potential to expend energy. Plenty of energy happening here at the moment, Damon. Possibly a little too much.'

'Breathe, Ruby.'

'I am. It's not helping. I really need to get rid of some of this energy *now*. You are so hot when you're hacking, by the way. Who knew?'

'The things I do for you,' he murmured, and swung her into an alleyway and pinned her against the wall, his mouth mere millimetres from her own. 'Settle down, Ruby.'

'Or what?' she whispered, just before she snaked her hand around his neck and drew him down for a hot, open exploration of his mouth. Plenty of energy happening between them at the moment. Enough tactile stimulation to make her forget her own name.

Damon groaned and the kiss turned incendiary. Energy released only now the concern was that they'd both go up in flames.

'You'll get us arrested,' he murmured, with a nip for her mouth as he wrapped his hand around her wrist, dragged it away from his neck and set them walking again. 'Time to get you home, Ruby. Now.'

'Authority has always *really* worked for me,' she said breathlessly and meant every word. 'Seriously, who doesn't love a man who knows how to take charge? An expert in his chosen field. How did you get into this field, by the way? I'm assuming it wasn't part of any school study curriculum.'

'It was something of a calling.'

'Ah. Junior hacker, were you?'

'Not now, Ruby.'

'I'm thinking school database, assessment marks in need of rearranging...'

'I was doing them a *service*. Pointing out the holes in the system.'

'Of course you were. How old were you at the time? Fourteen? Fifteen?'

'Twelve.'

'What a brat.' Two more steps and Ruby stopped dead. 'Damon, I think I've found a solution to the energy crisis. See that clothes shop on the other side of the road? It's open.'

'I see it,' he said. 'But isn't it a little Hello Kitty for you?'

'You mean it's a shop for teens? I can do teen wear.' Ruby nodded vigorously. 'I'm a felon. I can do anything.'

'Technically, you're only an accessory.'

'Wrong. The skills were yours but I think you'll find I'm a first-degree principal, which is what you intended all along. You had to draw me in. Make me part of it so that I wouldn't talk about it. Which I won't. Ever. When do I get the files?'

'You don't. You get to read through them when you're ready, take from them what you can and then I destroy them.'

'I'm ready,' she said, and the glance he cut her told her more plainly than words his thoughts on her readiness for anything.

'No, really. I am. I am fully aware that these are not the sort of files you want to have hanging around. I should look at them soon.'

'When you're ready,' he said, quietly inflexible. 'You're not ready.'

'It's this heady life of crime. It's frying my brain.'

'It'll pass.'

'The pertinent question still being *when*?'

'Soon.'

'You have no idea how *alive* I feel at the moment,' she said. 'Do you feel alive too?'

'Yes.' With more than a hint of amusement about him.

'Does it ever get old for you? The ha—your work?'

'No,' he said and finally his smile came wide and unguarded. 'No, this never gets old.'

They made it back to Ruby's apartment eventually. Damon insisting they only take a short train hop and then a taxi the rest of the way home. Perhaps he wanted to make sure no one was following them and a tail was easier to spot in a taxi, but Ruby didn't ask and Damon didn't say. She asked him if he wanted a drink once they reached the kitchen—manners, Ruby—and when he said yes she asked what would he like and he said Scotch if she had it.

'Good choice,' she murmured and poured one for herself too, before setting a bowl of peanuts on the counter, and eyeing the backpack he'd placed on the stool next to him with a mixture of apprehension and longing.

'I may not be ready, Damon, but there's no way in hell I'm going to settle until I know what those files say about my father,' she told him, and he nodded and unzipped the pack and pulled out the computer and set it up to go before turning the computer around to face Ruby.

'Have at it.'

'Okay, Ruby,' she said more to herself than anyone else. 'You can do this.'

And opened the first file.

Fifteen minutes later she was none the wiser as to where her father was or what had happened to him.

'The bank's investigation team got called off by the FBI. The Feds referred it to the British, and as far as British Intelligence is concerned they're not pursuing it at all. And what the hell is an A48?'

'Road map co-ordinates?' Damon offered. 'The AK 47's second cousin? A road in Britain?'

'Is it really?'

'I think so.'

'Maybe he's there,' she said glumly and handed him the computer. 'Read them or delete them. There's precious little there that I didn't already know.'

'We can search again.'

'No,' said Ruby emphatically. 'I don't think I could stand it. I did what you asked of me, Damon, and I don't regret it but I certainly don't ever want to do it again. I'm a felon but I'm free. I haven't found my father but at least no one's found him dead. That's *good* news. I'm willing to embrace the no-news-is-good-news policy today. As for you and me...' Ruby's whiskey-coloured eyes reflected a guardedness he'd never seen in them before. 'I overheard something I shouldn't have about you, Damon, and I paid the price and now we're square. Aren't we?'

'Yes.' They were square.

'And as much as I've enjoyed getting to know you, the work you do scares me, Damon, and the life you lead you lead alone. I will think of you with pleasure and I will think of you with hunger but it's time for you to leave.'

'Hunger?' he queried softly.

'Don't dwell on it,' she told him wryly. 'Hunger's manageable. You're not.'

He knew it. 'Mind if I get changed? My suit's in your bathroom.'

'Chameleon.' But she said it with a smile. 'Go. Get changed. Break my heart all over again when you come back out wearing a Savile Row suit and a gotta-be-going smile. I'm a felon. Tough. Worldly. Brave. I can handle it.'

She was making it easy for him again. Easy for him to do what he knew he should do. Walk away.

Just him and a hatful of regrets.

'I'm heading to Australia in three days' time,' he said.

'Enjoy.' She didn't know why he was telling her this and it showed. Time to enlighten her.

'Come with me.'

'Pardon?'

'Come with me.' Nothing but impulsiveness on his part and astonishment on hers. 'I have a house on the beach and a few weeks free. You could stay there while you figure out what it is you want to do next. We could just…swim.' Or sink.

Probably the latter.

Ruby eyed him narrowly. 'You just want to keep an

eye on me. Make sure I don't go spilling your secrets where I shouldn't. You're obsessing about me knowing what it is you do.'

'Only a little.' Only a lot.

'Well, stop it or you'll go blind,' she told him heatedly. 'You. Can. Trust. Me. Which is more than I can say for you.'

He took a step towards her and watched her scramble off her barstool fast and put out a hand as if to ward him off. 'Damon,' she began warningly. 'We are so close to finishing this. Don't mess with the plan.'

'There's a plan?' Damon reached out and touched her hair, wove silken strands of it around his fingertips, and finally, as if she would break beneath his touch, set his lips to the edge of her mouth. 'Come with me,' he whispered. 'Forget the plan.'

'You scare me, Damon.' But she kissed him as if she was starving for him and he kissed her and knew he was insatiable for her in return.

'I'll try not to.'

'And you'll fool me into thinking that you care.'

'Maybe I do,' he whispered and slid his hands to her buttocks and picked her up, and she wrapped her legs around him and made him groan. 'Come with me.'

Fifteen minutes later, as she climaxed round him for the second time, he said, 'Ruby, *please*.'

And she said, 'Yes.'

CHAPTER EIGHT

DAMON tried to slip back into his father's apartment un-noticed. No chance of that with two older sisters sitting in wait for him as they watched whatever they were watching on the TV. That was the problem with sisters who'd done double duty as substitute mothers over the years—they saw everything. Especially those things he didn't want them to see.

Poppy spotted him first as Lena was sitting with her back to the door, but Lena turned around and called him over and offered him a glass of wine.

No point trying to avoid them for they'd only follow him, so he anteed up and he sat his butt down.

Lena would take point, she always did, but only a fool would discount the effectiveness of Poppy when it came to stripping him bare.

Lena waited until he had his wineglass in hand and his thoughts in order before starting in on him, which meant she was either very tired or going soft.

'So,' she said, and fixed him with the mother stare. 'You and Ruby Maguire?'

'So?' he said in turn. 'Neither of us are in another relationship. Why shouldn't we?'

'You've known her for all of *two days*.'

'Five.'

'Does she know what you do?' asked Lena caustically.

'Well, she does *now*,' he replied in kind. 'Which part of *later* did you not understand?'

'Which part of stop being so bloody secretive do *you* not understand?'

'It's just habit.'

'No, it's a convenient way of keeping people at a distance, is what it is. Your whole way of life is designed to keep people away. Even family. Even me. I won't have it.'

'I'm getting that.'

And all of a sudden Lena looked close to tears.

'We failed you, didn't we?' she murmured. 'Jared and Poppy, and me. We let you pull away, and stay away, for far too long and now you can hardly find your way home.'

'I'm home,' he said desperately. 'I'm right here.'

But she shook her head and the smile she sent him was strained. 'No more lies, Damon. Not when it comes to Jared and whatever you might find out about him. Promise me.'

He did not want to promise that. 'Lena, I—'

'Promise.'

'All right.' He shook his head. 'All right, I promise. Satisfied?'

'Not quite,' she said as if moving on to the next insurmountable object. 'What happened with Ruby?'

'Nothing much.' Give or take a momentous decision or two.

'Can you trust her?'

'Put it this way, if I can't, I'm f—'

'Got it,' said Poppy primly and he and Lena shared a smile of amusement.

'Good,' he said blandly and set his wine down on the coffee table. 'Is that it for the interrogation?'

'Not quite,' said Poppy and Damon sighed. Poppy's turn.

'How much do you like her, Damon? Maybe this un-anticipated openness with Ruby can be a good thing. Room—if you want it—for a relationship to grow.'

'No,' he said. 'What would I do with a relationship? Besides destroy it. Drag Ruby around the world with me? Pull her into the life? No.' He stared broodingly at his wineglass. 'Ruby started out as a distraction, nothing more. Now she's even more of a distraction, but as for anything permanent? No.'

'That's three nos in a row,' murmured Lena. 'That's a lot of nos.'

'She's coming to the beach house with me,' he offered reluctantly. No point trying to hide it. They'd find out soon enough.

'That's interesting,' said Lena. 'Has Damon ever taken a woman to the beach house to your knowledge, Poppy?'

'No.'

'No. That's two more nos, just in case anyone's counting.'

'I have to be able to trust her,' he said grimly.

'So how does that work?' asked Lena. 'You're just going to keep her there until you do? Could take a life-time, Damon. Knowing you.'

'I think it's a good idea,' said Poppy. 'Give them more

time to adjust to Ruby knowing that little bit more about
Damon than she should. Besides, the trust will come.
I'm sure of it.'

Poppy was a sweetheart and an optimist. Damned if
Damon knew how she'd come to be part of this family.

'And maybe we can help. Maybe if we sat down with
Ruby over a drink or two and some girl talk we could
make it seem more…normal. Nothing to concern her.
You never bring your work home. You never let us near
it. You're really very noble and protective where that's
concerned.'

'I took her hacking with me,' he said curtly.

'You what?' said Poppy incredulously.

'You *idiot*,' said Lena.

And the conversation was mostly downhill from
there.

A week and a half later Ruby made her way to Sydney
and from there to Ballina near Damon's house on the
coast. Her work for Russell was done. She'd left the little
cat in the care of her next-door neighbour's six-year-old
daughter in exchange for letting her neighbour's parents
use her apartment during their two-week holiday stay in
Hong Kong. It was an arrangement that seemed to suit
everyone, including one tiny standoffish cat.

Nothing to hold her in Hong Kong now and nothing planned except for a week or two of sand, sea and
Damon, and she didn't know what to expect from him,
other than surprises. She didn't know why she was here
except that somewhere between meeting him and agree-
ing to this, she'd lost her brain.

What kind of woman flew halfway around the world

to visit a man who'd enchanted her and then warned her not to expect anything from him? A man for whom secrets and hacking and blackmail were everyday events? Or at least regular events.

Why had she *ever* said yes to this?

You're in love with him, said a little voice but Ruby rejected the notion outright.

I am not!

Then you're besotted by him, said the little voice, and this much she had to concede.

The sex is very good, yes.

You're going to try and change him. Turn him into a good boy.

Not sure that's possible. Anyway, he's not entirely bad. Espionage is a time-honoured profession. Heroic even.

He's a thief, Ruby.

He works to preserve the power balance between nations. He aims to protect. He was trying to protect *me* from the consequences of knowing too much. That's very honourable.

Silence from the stalls.

Win for Ruby.

But as she stepped through the arrival doors of the small regional airport and spotted Damon and her body melted and her wits turned to water with nothing but a glance from those midnight-blue eyes, the little voice spoke again.

You are so utterly gone on this man. Accepting him for what he is. Defending his less-than-stellar decisions. Not even wanting to tweak him. Put your own life on hold just to be with him. What's that if not love?

It's not *love*. It's just…exploration.

And you're irrational. Ladies and gentlemen of the jury, I rest my case.

But Ruby wasn't listening any more, she was too busy walking towards Damon.

He stood well back from the crowd, with his back to a wall and his hands in the pockets of a pair of calf-length cargos. He looked more tanned than he had been at Christmas. His white T-shirt—like his cargos—had seen better days.

Beach wear, one supposed. Casual and comfortable.

Ruby's wardrobe rarely ran to casual, comfortable beachwear. Tennis garb on Rhode Island was about as casual as she got. Mainly because, without fail, across all the years of her upbringing, she'd never not been on show. At her father's side. As her mother's daughter. Appearances mattered.

She had a feeling that appearances didn't matter much to Damon.

'I like your headband,' he said when he reached her.

Or maybe they did.

'It's very restrained for you,' he said next.

Which was true, because she'd gone for a plain white band to match her uncrushable white travelling shirt and jacket and her equally uncrushable lemon-coloured miniskirt. Sometimes synthetics were the only way to go.

'I like your tie,' she said in return, and his eyes warmed and he leaned down to greet her with a casual kiss, the kind that got bandied about between friends.

'You came,' he said next. 'I wasn't sure you would.'

And suddenly the air between them crackled with everything they *weren't* saying.

'I said I would.'

'Still...' Damon shrugged. 'People change their minds.'

'Have you?' Best to get it over with, if Damon had indeed changed his mind about the wisdom of her visiting him here.

'No,' he said quietly. 'I'm in if you are.'

'I'm here,' she said simply. 'And I'm not here under duress.'

Damon's smile came slow and sweet. 'Welcome to Australia, Ruby. How are you liking it so far?'

'Sydney Harbour's far more beautiful than in its pictures and the vibe so far is—' she spared a glance for his superbly fitting T-shirt '—relaxed. I may not have packed the right clothes.'

'Lucky for you we have shops. Or you can just borrow some of mine.'

'You mean you have more than one set?' she queried archly.

'I have a few sets at the house. C'mon, let's get you there. From there we'll hit the beach. You'll like the beach.'

Damon's vehicle was some sort of utility four-wheel drive. Unprepossessing. New-car clean. Nothing to write home about.

His beach house, on the other hand, completely enchanted her. Split level, the rooms wrapped around a central Balinese-style pavilion area, and the ceilings soared, and windows were everywhere.

There were guest rooms and games rooms, sitting

rooms and entertainment halls. An open-plan chef's kitchen and a garden that offered lushness and privacy and invited exploration. A narrow path ran from the other side of the outdoor pool, over a smattering of sand dunes, and wound its way down to the beach. The beach stretched for miles on either side, waves crashed ebulliently on the sand, and the ocean beyond the waves stretched clear to the horizon.

Casual, comfortable living didn't *come* any more luxurious than this.

'It's beautiful, Damon,' she said as he set her luggage down and turned towards her.

'It's easy to kick back here,' he said quietly. 'Be as formal or as informal as you like. As elegant or whimsical as you like.' He offered up a tiny smile. 'Just be yourself. This house will hold you; enjoy whatever you bring to it, even. And so will I.'

Now *there* was a welcome to set a heart to fluttering. She'd forgotten just how easily he could charm her when he wanted to. 'You speak as if this place is alive.'

'It is. The minute I walked through its doors I knew I had to own it.'

'Impulsive.'

'Or maybe I just know what I want.'

'Well, there's that too.' And she couldn't fault it.

'If you find any girl stuff here, it's Lena's,' he said. 'She's been staying with me up until a couple of days ago.'

'Got it. Thanks for the heads up,' said Ruby. 'How is Lena?'

'Frail. Not nearly as strong as she wants to be.'

'She didn't strike me as weak, Damon. Even in Hong Kong. Begs the question of what she used to be like.'

'Amazing,' he said simply. 'She was amazing. She sends her regards, by the way, and she left you a basket full of bath stuff and creams for you to use during your stay. It's in your room.'

'I'll have to thank her.'

'There's a housekeeper who comes in a couple of times a week. I had her prepare a bedroom for you.'

'Oh,' said Ruby, and eyed him uncertainly. 'Thank you.'

'Doesn't mean I don't want you in my bed, Ruby. Just that there's a room you can call your own as well. I asked Lena if that was the sort of set-up you might prefer. She said yes.'

Lena said.

Thanks, Lena.

He headed towards a wide wooden bowl and dropped his keys in it and took something else out of it.

'I'm screwing this up, aren't I?' he said and ran a hand through his hair for good measure. 'It's just… I've never brought a woman here before. I wanted to do it right. Lena warned me not to push you into anything you weren't ready for. Apparently I can be a little too persuasive for my own good. I've also been ordered not to wear you out, get you sunburnt, drown you or take you hang-gliding.'

'Oh,' she said faintly. 'Hang-gliding.'

'You'll love it. Seriously.'

'Chances are I *won't*,' she murmured and Damon grinned. 'I'm a guest, Damon. You're meant to be indulging me, not trying to kill me.'

'Yeah, Lena mentioned that too. She also mumbled something about best behaviour, picking up wet towels, keeping regular sleeping hours and not gaming on the computers half the night, and, oh, she said to tell you good luck. Sisters are wonderful, aren't they?'

'I don't know, I don't have any,' she said smoothly. 'Are we done with the household warnings yet? Any locked rooms I must never enter? Broom cupboard I should never open?'

'By all means open the broom cupboard,' he murmured. 'Wouldn't want to deprive you of the joy of household chores.' His smile turned wry and his eyes grew serious. 'It's all right, Ruby. There's nothing here you can stumble over when it comes to my work. I never bring it home and I never let it touch the people around me. That time in Kowloon with you was the exception, not the rule. It won't happen again.'

'Fine by me,' she answered quietly, and turned her attention to her luggage and smiled up at him with a false sunshinery her mother would have been proud of. 'I bought a gift for your household,' she said, and withdrew from her hand luggage the duty-free Scotch and champagne she'd purchased at the airport. 'There's caviar *somewhere* in there too. I seem to have developed a taste for it. That would be your fault.'

Damon smiled and held something out towards her in return. 'For you,' he said.

It was a headband. A cluster of fresh frangipanis twined around a solid frame, only on closer inspection the frangipanis were made of porcelain.

'Oh, yes.' Ruby made no effort to hide her pleasure

as she slipped off her old headband and replaced it with the new. 'That'll work.'

It was then that he kissed her. A meeting of lips that came fleeting at first, and then he returned for more and this time he savoured her.

He did that, she remembered belatedly.

He had a way of sliding into a moment and savouring whatever it might bring.

'Well, hello,' she murmured when their lips parted. And thank God. 'I've been wondering where you were.'

'I was giving you space.'

'Little hint for when we next meet,' she said, and punctuated her remark with the rasp of her tongue across his lower lip. 'Presents are good, presents are wonderful, but as far as space is concerned…I don't need it.'

Ruby smiled and wove her hands through his hair and let him drag her against his hard, rangy body. 'Though I am very aware that I *do* need a shower,' she protested as he slid her jacket from her shoulders. 'I'm straight off the plane.'

'Contrary, Ruby.'

'Well, yes. Surely you hadn't forgotten already?'

He had such busy hands. They slid beneath her skirt, and the next thing she knew he'd leaned back against the low-slung sofa and lifted her up, and her knees were finding purchase on it the better to plaster herself against him.

Damon's thumb slipped between her panties and stroked.

Ruby gasped and he ate it straight from her mouth.

She pushed forward and they toppled over the back

of the sofa and onto the cushions and it didn't matter any more that she'd wanted to shower, she needed to feel Damon's touch on her skin and his lips caressing hers.

'I dreamed of you,' she told him as he ran his hands over her thighs and positioned her exactly where she wanted to be. 'You were lawless. Bad. And I wanted you even more because of it.'

He took her mouth again and this time his kiss held a hint of savagery in it. 'I have ethics,' he whispered. 'Boundaries. I can even be hospitable when I really put my mind to it. You'll see.'

His questing fingers slipped beneath the boundaries of her panties again and Ruby shuddered with need of less boundaries and more contact. He dipped a long finger inside her and Ruby gasped her pleasure and she held his hand in place and closed her eyes the better to concentrate on his touch.

'I dreamed of you, Damon. Lord, how I dreamed of you.'

'I dreamed of you too,' he murmured as she dealt with the buttons and the zip at his waist and took him in hand.

'What was I doing?' she whispered as she slid her panties aside and positioned him for entry.

'This.' His voice guttural as he surged up inside her, his hands at her waist, vicelike as he held her in place. He slowly withdrew, and then rocked up into her again. 'You were doing this.'

They swam in the surf much later in the day, and then showered together and she used the bubbles Lena had left for her on him, and after that he sat her down at the kitchen counter in her underwear and fed her a toasted BLT sandwich on sourdough with mayonnaise.

He was handy in the kitchen—not fussy about what he put together but competent nonetheless. He put things away when he was done with them. He knew where things lived.

Definitely a point of difference between Damon and the rest of the men in her life. Missing fathers and step-fathers and the like. Staff inhabited kitchens in their world—not them.

'Have you ever surfed before?' he asked her later that afternoon as they sat on the sand and watched the waves come crashing in.

'I've skied before,' she said lazily. 'I have very fond memories of a winter in Switzerland where I was a fear-less snowboard queen of the mountain.'

'I'm very impressed,' he said. 'Then what happened?'

'Then we went to live in Bahrain.' A fond sigh es-caped her. 'I learned to drive in Bahrain.'

'Please don't tell me you learned to drive in a racing car unless you want to see me weeping with envy.'

'Of course I didn't.' She stood up, brushed sand from her rear. 'I learned to drive in a Hummer in the des-ert. My instructor's name was Carl. Carl set my girlish heart aflutter with his commando impersonation but, alas, he wasn't much of one for reckless endangerment. Even in a Hummer.'

'Surfing could be a little sedate for you,' said Damon in reply. 'If the wind picks up this afternoon we'll break out the kiteboards.'

* * *

Surfing was not sedate. Nor was the kitesurfing they attempted later that afternoon. The hang-gliding they did the following day didn't qualify as sedate either. There was more swimming. More love-making. And for Ruby, plenty of naps and lazing about in between the next action-man adventure.

Damon didn't nap. Not ever. He slept well through the night—when they slept—and needed no rest whatsoever during the day.

He wasn't one for television unless it was as background to whatever else he happened to be doing at the time. He cooked. He charmed. He rarely sat still. Even when sitting in his computer room he did ten things at once and all of them at warp speed.

When he ate, he liked to do it standing at counters. He could do a restaurant meal—he'd managed it in Hong Kong and he managed it again when they went into Byron Bay for dinner one night—but it wasn't his preference.

If there was a pool nearby he'd be in it. A pool table in the room and he'd be at it. The ocean and the toys he took to it could hold him for hours. Making love could also garner his undivided and sustained attention.

For now.

A suspicion formed in Ruby's mind about the type of kid he'd been, based on the man he'd become. How hard it must have been to educate a boy who couldn't sit still and whose mind worked that much faster than anyone else's. How hacking would have been such a natural fit for him given he'd had to sit at a computer and cut a snail's pace through all the schoolwork anyway.

Damon's lifestyle choices made far more sense to her now. His work kept him focused, delivered up the adrenalin he craved and kept him on the move. New places, new people, a world's worth of distraction— chances were he needed all those things in order to be content, and always would.

Not a man to plan a settled, predictable life around, but then, he'd never once suggested doing so.

'You're hyperactive, aren't you?' she asked him one night as he put together a late-night fruit platter that neither of them wanted, and tried—with limited success—to watch a movie with her.

Damon shot her a wary glance before deciding that the platter needed some biscuits.

'That's one label,' he offered up finally. 'There have been others.'

'Like what?' And when he didn't reply, 'Let me guess. Intellectually gifted, easily bored and distracted, physically reckless. How am I doing so far?'

'You're very astute.'

'ADD?'

He wouldn't look at her. Had to dump a load of mango peelings down the garbage disposal instead.

She took that as a yes, and gave up on ever getting to the end of the movie. Time to leave the sumptuously comfy lounge and take her bare feet and her stripey boy-leg panties and vest over to the kitchen counter instead. His side of the counter, mind. They were way past having a bench in between them.

Mango slices had rapidly become a favourite snack of Ruby's. She selected one, ate it, and smiled when a freshly wet hand cloth landed with a splat on the bench beside her. 'Thank you.'

She'd need that later. It wouldn't do to have sticky hands once she started running them all over Damon's irresistible flesh.

'So how do you feel about flying to Sydney tomorrow for a couple of days' exploration?' she said next. Change of subject, after a fashion. No change of craving for this man detected. 'I hear there's a bridge there to climb. The internet tells me there's a racetrack on offer too. Maybe we can rustle up a car or two and a pair of willing instructors to ride shotgun and have ourselves a little wager on the outcome? I can't let all that experience on Bahrain's international circuit go to waste. Because I did get there eventually. I may not have mentioned that earlier. Memories of Carl weeping inconsolably over his Hummer's split gearbox casing may have distracted me.'

'You destroyed a man's gearbox?'

'Well, not on *purpose*. Good thing I was wearing my buzzy bee headband at the time, otherwise he may have taken one look at me and seen red.' She picked up another mango slice and offered it to him. 'Mango?'

'You don't have to scatter your conversation for me, Ruby. Or give me a hundred and one conversation threads to choose from. I can follow a one-track conversation just fine,' he said quietly. 'Labels and all. And, yes. Doctors diagnosed me ADHD as a kid.'

Ruby frowned. 'Were you medicated?'

'There was medication,' he said. 'Wasn't easy, getting me to take it.'

'Rebellious.'

'I didn't need it. I can control it. I can be still. You don't need to indulge me by offering up adventure trips to Sydney whenever you think I'm getting bored.'

He sounded irritated and looked defensive. Apparently this was contagious.

'Is indulging you such a sin?' she argued mildly. 'And here I thought it was part of being a good house guest. Sometimes I indulge you, sometimes you indulge me. And sometimes we leave each other alone. Given that you've been indulging my every whim for the past few days I figured it might be time to ante up.'

Ruby ate the mango piece, seeing as Damon's mouth was set in a tightly closed line. She wiped her sticky fingers down his shirtfront and pushed him aside so she could get to the tap and rinse her hands.

'I wasn't *judging* you, Damon. I'm trying to *understand* you, and every time I think I come close you put up another wall.' She rinsed her hands and shook the excess water off them with a decidedly annoyed flick, before turning around and running smack bang into a wall of simmering manhood. She poked a pointy finger into Damon's well-exercised chest. 'It's very irritating.'

'Is that so?' he said silkily.

'Yes.' Another poke for the immovable object. 'And stop trying to distract me with sex.'

'I thought you liked the sex.'

She loved the sex. She was fast approaching the conclusion that fighting with Damon and then making up with him could well lead to incandescently memorable sex. 'That is not the point.' Another jab, only this time he caught her hand and flattened it against his chest.

'What is it we're doing here, Damon? Getting to

know each other? Indulging in a no-strings-attached, short-term affair where getting to know each other better is not a requirement? Are you trying to decide whether you can trust me to keep your secrets? What? Because I can't play this game if I don't know the rules.'

'There is no game,' he said quietly and redirected her hand to his heart. 'No rules either. Just an automatic defence against a criticism I've worn my entire life.'

He could break her heart too, whenever he wanted to. Distract her so that she never pushed too hard when it came to the question uppermost on her mind. The 'where are we going with this' question. The 'what the hell am I still doing here when you won't even let me know the simplest things about you' question.

'I don't have *all* the symptoms of ADHD,' he said gruffly. 'I can focus when I want to. I think before doing. I can be still.'

'Really?'

'I can.'

'But you don't need to be, do you? You've organised your life so you don't have to be still, and that's fine too. Plenty of other people organise their lives that way too. I've spent my entire life surrounded by gifted, driven, workaholic risk-takers who wouldn't know how to rest or be still if their lives depended on it. Your father's one of them. My father was another. Stepfather number three too, although he enjoys coming home. That's what my mother does—she makes him enjoy coming home.'

'There are women who still do that?' He looked intrigued.

'Yes,' she said pleasantly. 'I'm not one of them. I want a career.'

'Couldn't you do both?' he murmured silkily.

'Could you?' she asked in kind. 'Would you?'

'We're circling the relationship question again, aren't we?'

'Yes.'

'Not sure I have that much to offer you, Ruby.'

Not what Ruby wanted to hear. 'I thought you might say that. This house, is it yours free and clear?'

'Yes.'

'Any others?'

'A downtown apartment in Massachusetts.'

'Nice. Any other dependants I don't know about? Ex-wives? Children? Goldfish?'

She'd won from him a tiny smile. 'No.'

'So apart from your work—which you never bring home—you're actually pleasantly unencumbered.'

'Are you judging my suitability as a *spouse*?'

'Yes. You seem to think you have little to offer in that department. I'm presenting an alternate view. Where were we? Ah, yes. Your family seems sane enough— the ones I've met. I'm going to give them a tick.'

'You just don't know them well enough yet.'

'How many times a week would you want to have sex?'

Damon blinked. Then he smiled. 'A lot. Surely that's a strike *against*,' he murmured silkily.

'Depends on the woman,' she offered in counter. 'The timing. The mood. I'm going to go out on a limb here and vouch for your expertise. How many times a week would you cook?'

'Depends where we were.'

'Good answer,' she said with a nod. 'Any health issues? Genetic peculiarities? Apart from the ADHD of course. That one's already noted.'

'No.'

'So far, so good, wouldn't you say?' she said and speared him with a glance. 'Alas, there is still your inability to let anyone ever get close to you to consider. That one's proving problematic.'

'Do tell.'

Oh, she intended to. But not right yet.

'You know it was my father who taught me how to judge people,' she said lightly. 'He made an art form out of figuring out what makes people tick. Discovering their weaknesses, testing their strengths. His verdict would be that you undervalue yourself, by the way. He'd wonder what the hell happened to make you so insecure about being you. Then he'd play you to his advantage, but that's a whole other story that I really don't want to get into right now. Suffice to say that he taught me well and that I know a little something about reading people. Judging them. Playing them, even, but that's a whole other story that we probably don't need to dwell on either.'

'Maybe later,' he said with a hint of his old smoothness.

'Maybe never,' she countered and his grin came quick and free.

'What is it you're trying to say to me, Ruby?'

'What I'm *trying* to say is that I may be judging you, Damon, but I do not find you lacking. You have many fine qualities. You have plenty to offer. What I'd also like to get on record is that I don't need any lavish promises from you. I don't necessarily need a spouse. But if you *are* interested in exploring some kind of continuing relationship with me I do have one demand.'

'You'd make a wonderful divorce lawyer,' he murmured. 'What is it?'

'I want you to let down your defences and let me see you. The real you. No obfuscation. No distractions. No best behaviour. Just you.'

He didn't seem to know how to take her words. What to do with them or say in return. Wary man. Heartbreakingly vulnerable man underneath all the layers.

'So… I'm about to get naked and wet in that gorgeous pool over there,' she said and sidestepped him neatly. 'Care to join me?'

Ruby didn't wait for Damon's reply, just headed poolside and started shedding clothes. She glanced back over her shoulder at him.

'You did say that if I ever wanted to win an argument with you all I had to do was get naked, right?'

'Right.'

Damon hardly recognised his own voice, it cracked and wavered like a pubescent boy's.

'You are so *hot* when you're being cautious,' she said with a siren's smile. 'Gives you a totally unfair advantage.'

'Says the naked woman standing in water up to her waist.'

'Just so,' she said archly. 'Why is your shirt still on?'

'Beats me.' He dragged it up and over his head. Let it drop to the ground.

'Better,' she murmured appreciatively. 'Shirtless and brooding is a good look for you. Almost as good as naked and lost in the moment. Want to come and lose yourself in the moment with me, Damon?' No teasing in her now, just a longing directed straight at him.

'I just did,' he said and went to join her.

CHAPTER NINE

HEADING Sydneyside suited Damon. He and Ruby could—and did—play hard here. They had a suite overlooking Circular Quay but they didn't spend much time there. Out and about was Ruby's preferred state of being while in Sydney and, for all that Damon often accompanied her, she had no problem heading one way and waving Damon in the other direction if their interests diverged.

She had a confidence he envied. She knew how to be herself, and it was a contrary and fascinating self indeed. *Never* sloppy in appearance. Analytical when it came to the behaviours of others. He could see her as a lawyer. She had the shrewdness.

And the capacity to argue either way.

'I mentioned you to my handler,' he said over breakfast on their third morning in Sydney. They were down at the Quay, sitting in a sidewalk café, with the sun shining brightly and another day of exploration in front of them, give or take a job interview for Ruby and a work appointment for him.

'You what?' said Ruby.

'I figured it was time I told him I wanted to see a bit more of you.'

'Much as I am bowled over by such a hugely romantic gesture, couldn't you have told me first?'

'I need to get back to work soon and I need to know how careful I'm going to have to be. I asked him if anyone had you under surveillance on account of your father and the chances that he might get in contact with you.'

'And what was the answer?'

'He said no. According to his sources—and they're extensive—you've never been under surveillance. Not even in the days following your father's disappearance.'

'Maybe they're understaffed,' she muttered sourly.

'Seems unlikely. He asked me if I wanted him to do some more digging about your father. I said I'd take care of it.'

'You already have.'

'I thought I might take another look. See if there's something I missed.'

'Like what?'

'I don't know yet.' But he was beginning to have his suspicions. 'Could your father have worked in intelligence?'

Ruby's surprise was instantaneous. 'Where did *that* come from?'

'The bank handed over an eight-hundred-and-seventy-two-million-dollar recovery investigation to the Feds, the Feds handballed it to British Intelligence and the British backed off. Maybe your father belongs to someone else. You've said more than once that he was a master at reading and manipulating people. A man who kept secrets. It'd fit.'

Ruby frowned and lifted her sunglasses to the top

of her head. The better to see him or the better for him to see her. Wordlessly demanding a more secure connection between them and getting it too. She was full of tricks like that.

'As far as I know, my father only ever worked in finance,' she said cautiously.

'Would your mother know if he'd ever been involved elsewhere?'

'I doubt it.'

'Might have been why she bailed.'

'No, that would be because of the infidelity and my father never being where he said he was going to be, or doing what he promised to do,' countered Ruby dryly.

'Must've been some childhood.'

'My father did his best to be there for me,' she said. 'Usually he succeeded. But not always. Enough, Damon. You're barking up the wrong tree. My father was a merchant banker not a spy.' She dropped a kiss on his cheek and made to leave his company for an appointment with the senior partner of an Australian-based law firm. 'I need to get to this appointment. I'll tell you about my woefully overprivileged upbringing another time.'

She kissed his other cheek and drew back to stare at him searchingly before offering up another kiss, this time for his lips. 'Be good. Don't dig. Not on my behalf. I have enough trouble accepting that you dig on behalf of other people.'

He accepted the kiss she placed on his other cheek with a faint smile.

'What happens if they offer you a job?'

'There is no job. I'm just fishing and so are they.'

Damon watched her walk away, admiring the sway of her hips and the curve of her slender calves. 'Let me see you. The real you,' she'd said to him only three days ago. Today she'd told him to be good and not dig. As far as he was concerned that was a bit like telling a shark not to swim.

Ruby would have a job offer within the hour, he predicted.

He'd have more information on her father within the hour too.

And then they would look at each other again and see what came of that.

Damon found another coffee shop and this one had everything he needed. He checked in with the home office, a routine ping and nothing more.

A different café next and another easy public access point and this time Damon turned his efforts to discovering somewhat more about Ruby's father and the missing millions. FBI records turned up a referral of the case over to the British Intelligence Service. Their records turned up nothing but dross.

On a hunch, he wormed his way into yet another database. Deeper and deeper still, as his coffee sat untouched on the table beside him, the painted wall at his back giving him all the privacy he needed. His senses stayed with the coffee crowd but he gave his mind over to the language in his head, and the pathways opening up for him on screen, no telling where they would lead.

The lure of the unknown, a siren song he'd never been able to resist. A failing, some would say, but he'd never been any different and if indeed it was a flaw, he'd done his damnedest to turn it into a useful one.

Two minutes in and no fixed destination in mind, just a name and a suspicion. A database to search through and eventually a hit. A record of employment, collated not by employer but by counterparts with a need to know. He sipped at his coffee as he waited for the download. Time enough to read it later.

This lot had a reputation for knowing when their security had been compromised. They wouldn't know who, and they wouldn't know what he'd been after once he'd had his way with the memory interface, but still…

Time to go.

He gave the waitress a smile, left a tip on the table…

He had an uneasy feeling about this one. A notion that he should have left this particular stone unturned, and it mixed with the rush of the run and made him want to lengthen his stride in the way of a man in a hurry.

Easy now, no problem here.

Just a little light reading for later on.

Ruby was already back at the suite when Damon returned just on lunchtime, several forms of transport behind him, his computer sporting some brand-new motherboard components and his reading up-to-date.

Fascinating reading. King hit on his maiden run. Knowledge was power and power was useful. Provided you knew how to wield it.

Damon far preferred leaving the wielding part of the process to others.

Problem: Harry Maguire had been a key asset for

the British Intelligence Service when it came to monitoring—and occasionally enabling—money laundering throughout South-East Asia. Why British and not American? No idea. Maybe they'd simply been the ones to get to him first. Regardless, he'd been on the payroll for over thirty years.

Thirty years. Before Ruby. During Ruby. And he'd never said a word.

Next problem: Harry had been monitoring a sensitive money-laundering deal when he'd disappeared. A deal the British had not wanted to see go through. General consensus had it that Harry was dead but no corpse had been forthcoming so nobody knew for sure.

Damon's immediate problem: what to tell Ruby?

Right now he was leaning heavily towards telling her nothing.

Ruby smiled when she saw him and indicated an already open bottle of champagne on the kitchenette counter.

'You got the job,' he said.

'I was offered the job.'

'Did you *take* the job?'

'I'm letting them know.'

'Where's it based?'

'Hong Kong.'

'Handy.'

'Not for someone who's looking to start afresh. My father cast a long shadow in Hong Kong, Damon, and not just because people think him a thief. I'm tired of tripping over it.'

Damon said nothing.

'I also wouldn't have access to the resources and

community a main office would offer,' she continued thoughtfully. 'Mentoring. A cohort to learn from, and with. They want me to fly solo in Hong Kong. I could do that for myself.'

'You could access the company's resources online,' he said mildly. 'Computer conferencing to take care of the mentoring and working together business.'

Ruby's eyes narrowed thoughtfully.

'Not that I'm trying to influence you. But it could be done. Leaving you with a certain autonomy when it comes to running things your way.'

'Why, Damon West. Are you calling me a dictator?'

'Course not,' he said with a shake of his head as he crossed to the counter and filled the champagne flute she'd left there for him.

'Liar.'

Damon grinned and tilted his glass her way. 'Here's to choices and what we make of them. Congratulations on being offered the job, whether you take it or not.'

'Thank you,' she said graciously and held out her glass for a refill. 'Don't mind me, I'm still debating the offer. I'll be debating the offer for days and your power to distract me will be fully tested. What did you get up to this morning in my absence?'

'Nothing much. Bit of sightseeing,' he said offhand.

'Ah.'

Ruby didn't ask for details. And Damon didn't say.

Damon took Ruby's preoccupation with career planning as a signal to do a little career expansion of his own. He acquired a contract to design a network security system for a corporate customer. Work that he could do from the beach house and make a start on straight away if Ruby didn't mind.

Ruby didn't mind. She'd decided to face the complexities of her burgeoning relationship with Damon on a day-by-day basis. No planning required. No stressing about her and Damon's future allowed.

Besides, the reality of Damon's work process was highly entertaining.

Damon worked in a room full of computers with half a dozen programs running at once, and he did it in ten-minute bursts while wearing board shorts and a tan.

Not exactly office-trained was Damon.

In the absence of a whole lot else to do, Ruby set her sights on conquering kitesurfing. Her stomach muscles would thank her once they'd stopped protesting, and Damon's work pattern meant that every fifteen minutes or so she could hand the rig over to him and take a break.

At which point her stomach muscles would thank her on the spot.

'Lunch time,' he said as he came down to meet her at water's edge for the umpteenth time that morning. 'And we have visitors.'

'Who?'

'Lena and Trig.'

'Trig for trigonometry?' she said as she unbuckled the harness, more than happy to be done with it for the day.

'Trig for trigger-happy,' he said, and unclipped the kite lines and gave her a breezy grin.

'Oh, that's comforting,' she murmured. 'Friend of yours?'

'Friend of Jared and Lena's, mainly. We grew up next door to each other. Jared and Trig joined the service together. Lena joined up a year later. Longest year of Lena's life,' said Damon. 'Mine and Poppy's too.'

'So has Trig heard from Jared?'

'No, but he's got a lead on where he might be.' They started up the beach, Damon loaded down with gear and Ruby's aching muscles happy to let him carry the lot.

'He's come to you for help?'

'Yeah, but not the kind of help you're thinking. Trig wants to depart on a little fact-finding mission. Lena's determined to go with him.'

'That doesn't sound like a particularly smart idea.'

'Can I quote you on that?'

'Only if you want me to wear Lena's everlasting animosity.'

'Point taken. I'll keep you in reserve, counsellor.' And then they were at the house pavilion and it was smiles and introductions and greetings, with Ruby acutely aware of her tangled hair and the salt on her skin.

Damon and Trig moved over towards the garden tap to rinse off the kite-surfing rig.

Ruby turned to Lena and thanked her kindly for the welcome-to-the-beach-house lotions and potions and then slid on into a polished how-do-you-do and a lovely-to-see-you.

'You're looking well,' said Ruby, a substantial exaggeration given Lena's extreme slenderness, but no woman needed reminding that she'd looked better yesterday. 'I, on the other hand, look like a hoyden. Give me five minutes to shower and change and I'll be back.'

'Take ten,' said Lena with a smile. 'The boys'll talk kite-board rigs for at least that long.'

'Leaving you to do what? Entertain yourself?'

'Leaving me to mock them,' said Lena. 'It's a pattern we're all familiar with. Go. Wash off the salt. Put on the visitor clothes—I can see you want to. Besides, Trig's already compared you to half the Victoria's Secret Angels. I want to see the look on his face when you do your corporate princess thing.'

'The corporate princess is gone,' said Ruby. 'I bought myself some beach clothes.'

'Should be interesting,' said Lena. 'One of these days you're going to have to give me some fashion advice. The compliments I get whenever I wear the clothes you bought for me have been amazing.'

'I have two words for you,' said Ruby. 'Persian Pink.'

'Never,' said Lena with a gamine smile that made her truly beautiful. Oh, the things people never saw when they looked in a mirror.

An *oomph* and a thump from somewhere over near the tap caught Ruby's attention and she turned to find Damon in possession of the garden hose, apparently intent on cooling the trigger-happy one down. Trig, in turn, seemed equally intent on gathering up the hose line and strangling Damon with it—both of them grinning like sharks. 'Are they always like this?'

'Not *always*. Trig probably shouldn't have been staring at your arse. I did warn him.'

'About my bum?'

'That Damon was serious about you.'

'What makes you say that?'

'You're here, aren't you? And Damon's all happy and relaxed on the inside as well as on the surface. That's rare.'

Ruby eyed Lena uncertainly. 'You can tell all that just by looking at him?'

'Can't you?' said Lena with the beginnings of a smile. 'Oh, all right. Maybe I'm imagining things. Seeing what I want to see. But he's certainly very possessive of you, and making no apology for it with Trig. That's an excellent sign of attachment. Damon protects what's his. Always has. Usually with a complete disregard for his own safety that can be scary to watch.'

Possessive. Serious. Lena's words whizzed by, with Ruby scrambling madly to keep up. *Disregard for own safety. Scary.* Ruby backing up to ask the obvious question. 'Possessive how? As in if I even look at another man sideways he'll strangle me, possessive?'

'Not quite, although I wouldn't say he'd be entirely *happy* were you to look at Trig sideways.'

Neither, it seemed, would Lena be happy. Ruby stifled a smile. 'Duly noted.'

'All I was meaning,' said Lena repressively, 'is that if you were ever in danger, Damon would protect you with everything he had, including his life. For example, he pulled Poppy out of a rip once, when they were little. Saw her in trouble and swam like a demon to get to her, got caught in it as well and then swam like two demons to get them out. I thought they were both going to die.'

'Brave though.'

'Made an impression, I'll give him that.' Lena eyed

her speculatively. 'Damon used to avoid his I'll-die-
for-you dilemmas by not laying claim to much. Wonder
what he's going to do now?'

'Hopefully, stay alive,' said Ruby dryly. 'As for your
claims about Damon laying claim to me, I think I'll just
tell you I have no idea what you're talking about and go
and have me that shower now.' Ruby took a step towards
the back of the house and then turned around to assess
once more the wrestling tangle of well-muscled limbs.
'They're not going to kill each other *now*, are they?'

'No, Damon knows Trig was only winding him up
by studying you. He's made his point. Now they're just
saying hello.'

'Right.' That was hello. 'Australian thing, is it?'

Lena just smiled.

Ruby returned to the fray some fifteen minutes later,
wearing a pretty little cropped and layered silk camisole, heavy on the plums and pinks, ivory hipster trousers, bare feet, and her purple butterfly headband. She'd
taken the time to blow-dry her hair and apply a touch
of make-up. Visitors were visitors after all. No need to
disrespect them by not making an effort.

Trig stared at her as she approached them, his grin
wide and his gaze unholy. Probably her lack of shoes.
Could be the butterfly.

Damon stared too, eyes narrow upon her bared mid-
riff.

'Looking a little possessive there, boyo,' Trig murmured to Damon.

'Just feeling my way,' responded Damon evenly, and

then went and spoiled all that lovely nonchalance by shooting Trig a dirty glare. 'You're not feeling *anything*.'

Ruby's smile widened. 'I just couldn't find a *thing* to wear,' she said to Damon when she reached them. 'You might have to take me shopping.'

'I am *so* impressed,' said the aptly named Trig. 'What else does she do? Besides bait you.'

'I could tell you but you'd weep,' said Damon, and turned to Ruby. 'We're trying to convince Lena to stay here and concentrate on getting better while Trig goes looking for Jared.'

Family politics. Never, ever—on pain of death—get in the middle of it.

Particularly if you weren't family.

'How's that working out for everyone?' she said cautiously.

'You're a lawyer. Reason with her,' said Damon.

Oh, yes. This was going to end well.

'So… I'm guessing we've moved past delicacy, in terms of approach?' asked Ruby.

'Delicacy's not something we employ around Lena,' said Trig. 'Lena considers it a weakness.'

Okeydokeythen. Ruby ignored Lena's mutinous expression in favour of asking the obvious question. 'Lena, in your honest opinion, will you slow Trig down?'

'No,' said Lena.

'YES.' This from an extremely frustrated Trig. 'Lena, you have no idea how much I worry about you these days. Stay here with Damon and Ruby. Get well. *Get out of my goddamn head!*'

'Why would I want to be in your head?' Lena yelled back. *'There's nothing in there but testosterone.'*

'I don't know, Damon,' said Ruby dubiously. 'She looks fighting fit to me.' And in a voice she knew would carry, 'How long did you say they'd been married?'

That stopped them.

Lena scowled. Trig glowered.

Damon headed for the fridge in order to hide his smirk and returned with two beers and a bottle of white wine. 'I'll get glasses.'

Ruby smiled. Delicately. And watched him go. Watched him return and pour wine for Lena and slide it across the countertop, and pour one for her too, before distributing the beer. While the silence droned on.

'Far be it from me to want to take charge of this discussion,' she began calmly, and suffered Damon's extremely level gaze in silence, 'or take sides, but, Lena, it does seem to me that the gentlemen have a point. What if you end up having to move quickly because you're in danger? What if you have to run? Could you?'

Trig opened his mouth to say something. Ruby silenced him with a glance. 'Lena?'

'I can run,' said Lena in a thin hollow voice.

'Lena, you can barely *walk*,' countered Trig savagely. 'Don't you dare downplay your injuries to me. I was the one who pushed your *guts* back into your body.'

'I can run,' said Lena. And then went and spoiled her insistence with a fat and silent tear.

Trig fled, taking his beer and Damon with him. Out to the barbecue area where they set about unearthing a four-foot stainless-steel barbecuing wonder from its coverings.

'Looks like they're starting lunch,' said Ruby.

'I'm sorry,' said Lena as she wiped her tears away

with her fingers only to have more replace them. 'I'm not myself. I just want—'

'To be yourself again and find your brother. I know.' Ruby reached across the counter, covered Lena's hand and squeezed. 'It's okay.'

'No, it's *not* okay,' said Lena. 'I never cry. Especially not in front of Trig.'

'Because... Why not?'

'Because he'll never let me live it down.'

'Oh, I don't know,' said Ruby. 'Looks like a man hell-bent on forgetting the past few minutes to me. You want to know what else I think?'

Rhetorical question.

'I think you're terrified you might not recover from your injuries as well as you might like, and I think those two clowns out there are terrified right along with you. I think that regardless of what you want to do, what you *need* to do is take it easy on your body and listen to the clowns for once.'

Ruby smiled and the circus continued. 'Besides, Trig's not going anywhere unless you agree to stay here. I'm guessing he's saving that little titbit up for when all other forms of persuasion fail. What would you rather have him do, Lena? Babysit you or go look for your brother?'

Trig left. Lena stayed. And the following morning Ruby began to turn her mind to her future. Her two weeks were almost up and, much as she'd delighted in them, she couldn't stay on here indefinitely and neither would Damon.

Charming he remained, but Damon was getting restless.

The system design work he'd taken on currently held his attention but Ruby was under no illusions that he was about to forgo his covert work and his travelling lifestyle and become a model citizen. The jobs Ruby had taken to looking at all required her to commit to a particular course of action and stick to it. They all expected her to base herself somewhere for two to three years and stay there.

Ruby pushed the latest company structure and advancements file she'd been reading away from her with a sigh. Lena was at the kitchen bench making fruit smoothies for them both. Lena did not like being coddled and she'd just finished a workout in the pool that had left Ruby quietly terrified that Lena was going to overdo it and land herself back in hospital.

'I'm no medical expert,' said Ruby as Lena walked slowly towards the table, a smoothie in each hand. 'But have you considered that doing physio three times a day when the doctor recommends you only do it once might be doing you more harm than good?'

'Stop fussing,' said Lena. 'I'm fine. But seeing as we're being reflective, have you considered where Damon fits into all these work options you're contemplating?'

'Why do you think I'm rejecting them all?' Ruby took a glum sip of her smoothie. 'Have you any idea how hard it is to make plans that will accommodate your brother in my life?'

'Well, have you tried making them *with* him? That might help.'

'Ow,' said Ruby. 'Sarcasm. Don't you think that if I'd wanted to engage Damon on the topic I'd have done so already?'

'Maybe. Maybe not,' said Lena. 'You might be waiting for him to say *I love you*. Which he does, by the way.'

'And you know this how?'

'Observation.'

'I see,' said Ruby dryly.

'The thing is, Damon spends a lot of time thinking he's not worthy of love,' continued Lena earnestly. 'Pushing it away. He might not know how to say it. He might have to follow your lead. And you can lead, Ruby. You're very good at it.'

'Are you suggesting that I say it first?'

'That's exactly what I'm suggesting.'

'I'll keep it in mind,' said Ruby coolly. 'As long as *you* bear in mind that *I love you* is not an easy thing to say—and mean—no matter who's doing the talking.'

'I've overstepped my boundaries, haven't I?'

'You have.'

'Sorry. Bad habit.' Lena looked dismayed.

'You're here. The relationship is playing out in front of you and you want to smooth your brother's way. You're forgiven,' said Ruby, and meant it. 'But let me give you a little background information about me and the way I was raised.

'My father was a man of many secrets and even more agendas, none of which I was privy to. I loved him but I didn't know him. I adored him but I was never quite sure when he was being truthful and when he was lying through his teeth. Hell, I don't even know if he loved me. If he's alive and well and living off a mountain of stolen money and has no intention of contacting me ever again, I'm going to have to go with no.'

'That's quite a background,' said Lena with a grimace.

'Now enter Damon,' said Ruby. 'A fascinating, complex, glory of a man with a head full of secrets and a job that requires him to keep them. A man so used to keeping people *out* that getting him to reveal even the tiniest thing about himself requires a patience and perseverance I'm not sure I possess. And then just when I think I can't do this, he turns around and bares his soul for me—not his secrets but his soul, and I get lost in him, Lena, so lost it scares me. And he gets lost in me.'

Ruby's headband came off, and this time she left it off as she ran her hands through her already beach-swept hair.

'If this is love, it's not a comfortable, easy love,' she said. 'If this is honesty, it's going to take some getting used to.' Lena's sympathetic gaze cut to some place just over Ruby's shoulder. 'And if that's Damon I'm going to freak.'

'I just remembered a doctor's appointment,' said Lena. 'A really long one.'

'Lena.' Damon's quiet, measured voice confirmed the worst. 'No need to get up, though it'd be nice if you'd butt out.'

He came into view, a dangerously attractive man wearing long shorts and a simple grey cotton T-shirt that looked anything but simple on him. He held out his hand to Ruby, his ocean eyes stormy. 'Walk with me.'

It wasn't a request.

They headed for the beach path, Damon leading and Ruby in his wake once they got there, but he did not let her hand go and he did not slow his stride. He kept walking once they reached the water's edge.

Walking off a mad, one of her favourite nannies-of-old would have said. Better a walk than broken toys. And once Ruby had finally calmed down enough to be coherent, she'd say, 'Okay, Ruby Lou, talk. Who's wounded you most mortally now?'

That particular question had always been a prelude to a conversation about anger and wilfulness and how to manage both. The nanny would bring out her sewing kit and together she and Ruby would analyse the insult and Ruby's reaction to it and at the end of the conversation there would be a funny, pretty headband for Ruby Lou to wear.

'What can't you have?' Nanny Laura would say as the headband went on.

'My way all the time.'

'And why can't you have it?'

'Because other people have feelings too.'

'There's my considerate girl.'

A memorably grounded nanny, that one, though she hadn't lasted long.

But the lesson had sunk in and Ruby did her best to think of other people's feelings too.

Damon had feelings, ones that ran fathoms deep.

And Ruby had wounded them.

'How much did you hear?' she asked when they were halfway along the beach and the silence had reached suffocation point.

'Damon, stop. Please.' She planted her feet in the sand at the water's edge and tugged on his hand. 'I'm asking you to stop walking while I explain.'

She felt the pull of his hand against hers and held on tight. He could do this. Be still for her. And she could try and mend the damage done. 'How much did you hear?'

'All of it, Ruby.'

He turned to look at her, and she could see that exercise hadn't calmed him down any.

'All of it. Starting with my sister trying to explain away my faults and finishing with you saying you're too scared to take a chance on me.'

'I didn't say that,' argued Ruby. 'I said I needed time. There's a difference. I *am* taking a chance on you, Damon. What do you think I've been doing? I'm just not sure what happens next, that's all, and I'm not pushing you for answers. Dammit, Damon! You've made no mention whatsoever about where you're going or what you plan to do once these two weeks are up. You're playing us day by day and close to the chest and so am I. Isn't that what you *want*?'

Damon smiled mirthlessly. 'Apparently not.'

'Then what *do* you want? Because I'm willing to have this conversation if you are. I just didn't want to be the one to start it.'

'I want to talk about what comes next,' he said gruffly. 'Where you're going. Where you want to go. The things I have to do and the things I can change to suit myself. Or suit us.'

Damon took a deep breath and reached out to tuck a flyaway strand of hair behind her ear. 'No headband.'

'I left it on the table.'

'I know love and trust doesn't come easy to you, Ruby. It doesn't come easy to me either. But I do want to be with you. Make some changes so that I *can* be with you, at times. If that would suit you.'

It was a start.

CHAPTER TEN

THREE days later, on the back of some rather haphaz-
ard planning, Ruby went back to Hong Kong. Damon
joined her a week later. Living with her, loving her, and
watching her try and make up her mind on a new career
path and permanent location with a smile on his face
and a patience that surprised her.

When she'd gone round in circles a few times he
weighed in with reasoned argument.

If she liked it in Hong Kong why not stay on here for
a while?

Forget her father's actions, they were not hers to own
and if people couldn't see that they were fools.

At least in Hong Kong she already knew who her
friends were. The ones who'd stood by her when things
had gone bad. The ones who kept in contact with her
and valued her company.

An advantage over starting afresh, he'd said.

He could see things very clearly when he wanted to,
could Damon. Ruby's respect for him grew, along with
her dependence on making decisions *with* him rather
than without.

Eventually, she decided to make Hong Kong work for
her for now. The Australian-based law firm still hadn't

filled their Hong Kong position. Plenty of room now for some negotiation of terms. One week every month a trip back to the Sydney office to consolidate the work. Formalised mentorship facilitated by computer conferencing technology. And free rein to do things her way when it came to setting up shop.

And if the decision sounded as if it was based in part on Damon's solid reasoning that Hong Kong would prove a useful base for them both, well, maybe it was.

Damon too was looking to rent office space in Hong Kong. Build up a legitimate network development service for small businesses. Employ a manager. A couple of technicians. Lend a hand every now and then. Keep his head in the game. Go legit with at least some of his work.

It sounded good in theory.

Whether he would have enough focus to actually step up and *do* it was anyone's guess.

Days whizzed by and Ruby took to talking to the cat again.

A vastly friendlier little cat, for little girls were apparently very good at sneaking through a little cat's reserve. The cat, who now went by the name of Jao, now had two homes to choose from, and one he retreated to when he wanted peace and solitude and the other home he favoured when he wanted to play.

Not bad for a no-name scrap of mistrust and misery.

'Fall on your feet, don't you?' she told Jao, who'd developed a habit of taking a fast and clawless strike at her ankles from beneath the overhang of the kitchen bench. 'Just like Damon.'

Damon who'd been looking at office space but neglecting to pay attention to the contractual leasing terms of the office space chosen. Damon didn't have the patience for it. Ruby did. Also a vested interest in not wanting him to expire of frustration before his venture into the world of small-business ownership had even begun.

'Damon's going to need a *very* switched on business manager,' she said to the little cat as she marked for signing the leasing arrangement he'd decided to go with.

'Damon's well aware of that,' said a voice, and Ruby looked up from the papers and saw Damon coming towards her, fresh from the shower with only a towel to keep him company.

'You couldn't afford me,' she said, and favoured him with a very appreciative smile. 'Besides, I've decided to take the Hong Kong job. Even if I only do the initial set-up and then pass the position on to someone else. That corner suite we looked at yesterday would be perfect.'

'The ground-floor corner office with the too big reception area, too small a workshop and the little courtyard? The one you told me was on the border of Triad territory?'

'Yes,' said Ruby serenely. '*Border* being the operative word. Between *two* opposing Chinese corporations, actually. Authorities tend to steer clear and that is of benefit to a lawyer with a client base of asylum seekers, many of whom have not had pleasant experiences with authority.'

'Get each side to throw in a day guard and lockdown parking facilities for your wheels and I might even agree,' he said as he picked up the pen and scrawled his signature beside every cross. 'You'll be dealing with desperate people, Ruby. You're going to have to take precautions.'

'I know. And later on I want to pick your brains when it comes to securing computer files and whatnot. Maybe I can be your first customer.' She picked up the paper-work and waved it in his face. 'Next time, *read* it.'

'Why? You already have.' He dropped a kiss on her lips and forestalled further comment. 'You know, you're lucky to have me. I haven't mentioned locking you up and not letting you out of this apartment ever again *once* during this conversation.'

'Nor will you if you have any sense of fair play at all. When it comes to courting danger, each to his own.'

'The family's going to say it's my fault you went dark side,' he continued morosely. 'They'll say I encouraged you.'

Ruby smiled. 'And they'd be right. Am I going to have to get undressed in order to win this argument?'

'You've already won it. Besides, I need to change the topic,' he murmured, and let his bottom lip drag against hers before sliding his lips across to her ear. 'I have to go to Eastern Europe for work.'

Ruby drew away swiftly and fixed him with an un-friendly gaze. 'I *knew* you were buttering me up for something.'

'No, you didn't. You thought I was just being my usual charming self.'

This was true. Not that she had any intention of say-ing that aloud. '*When* are you going to Eastern Europe?'

'Today.'

Ruby nodded. Thumped him in the chest with a none-too-gentle fist. 'How long have you known?'

'Ten minutes.' He glanced at the microwave clock. 'Fifteen.'

'When are you coming back?'

'A week?' Damon shrugged. 'It's hard to say. Hopefully a week.'

'Will you call and let me know?'

'No contact. You know how this goes, Ruby. We've talked about it.'

Yes, but talking wasn't doing. Ruby glared at him afresh. 'Make sure you bring me back a present. At least then I'll know I've been in your thoughts.'

'A headband?'

'Yes,' she said and lifted her chin. 'A headband for reasonable, considerate, loveable little Ruby, and I'll give you fair warning. Regardless of my *inherently* forgiving nature, I do have a temper, and certain actions have been known to trigger it.' Her hands had gone to her hips. 'Keep your secrets when it comes to your work, I don't want them. As for our personal affairs, I don't like being manipulated and I resent being lied to. Are we clear?'

'Ruby, you're the classiest and most effective manipulator I've ever seen. How come I can't even *practise* on you?'

'I'm not joking, Damon. Don't ever play me that way.'

'I won't.'

'Promise me.'

'Ruby, I won't.'

And Ruby believed him.

Another week. No word from Damon, but then he'd warned her not to expect it. Ruby stayed busy and somewhere along the way she realised she wasn't fretting about Damon and the things he might be doing. Shades of grey and each to their own, and Damon would go about making the world a better place his way and Ruby would try and make the world a fairer place her way, and who was to judge which was the right way?

If Damon ever wanted a muse when it came to his work and the ethics involved he would get one. Label him a hero or brand him a thief. She could argue either way.

Ruby leased the corner office suite. Made a few changes. The walls would not be grey but ivory. The furnishings would be comfortable and not pretentious. Her new neighbours wondered what she was up to. She had flyers printed up listing the company's services. Obtained flyers and posters from charities and services that she thought her future clients would find useful. Word got around. Her new landlord stopped by.

Yes, she was Harry Maguire's daughter.

No, she had no idea where the money was, or her father for that matter.

Yes, she was opening up a law office specialising in migration, and yes, indeed, she would be most interested in having the local security service stop by her offices on their nightly rounds. Day rounds too, if they existed. It would be money well spent.

And Damon stayed away.

Day three of week two of his absence and Ruby's office walls were now ivory and she'd moved on to furnishings. Work desks and office chairs. A wooden table and benches and potted greenery for the courtyard. She started the hunt for a receptionist. At least three languages, she told the dressmaker three doors down. With written proficiency in two. Preferably someone who lived locally but wasn't closely affiliated with any of the Triads.

The dressmaker knew of someone who might be interested in part-time work. Very smart boy. The son of one of her regular clients. Chinese Korean.

And then just like that, Damon was back. Standing in the doorway of her new office, a bunch of purple orchids in one hand and a gaily wrapped package in the other.

'Two presents,' he said. 'I thought I might need them.'

'So true,' she said, and then Ruby was in his arms and Damon was twirling her round and kissing her with an intensity that belonged to him alone.

'Miss me?' he whispered when she finally broke free.

'Like crazy.'

'Feel like taking the afternoon off?'

'Only if you can get two desktop computers, a scanner/printer/fax and a notebook here and set up by nine tomorrow morning.'

Damon handed her his tributes and pulled out his phone. Two minutes later it was organised.

'Tell me you're impressed,' he said.

'Show off.' But she kissed him again and it was quite

some time before she turned her attention to the opening of gifts. 'I could get used to this.'

'That's the plan.'

'Truffles from Belgium,' she said in approval of the exquisitely boxed handmade selection. 'Very nice.'

'And this,' he said, and dangled a heart shaped pendant on a silver ribbon from his fingertips. Silver filigree that swirled an intricate path around a heart of red Murano glass.

'Damon, it's gorgeous,' she said with unfeigned enthusiasm and set about putting it on. 'Venice?'

'Still full of bridges and rising water.' He fingered the pendant at her neck. 'Guess what I discovered when I walked through the door and you looked up and smiled at me as if Christmas had come early?'

'That I like presents?'

'That Lena was right about one thing and wrong about another.'

'Lena's right and wrong about a lot of things. Which things are we talking about?'

'Love,' he said quietly, his gaze intent on hers. 'I love you, Ruby. And you don't have to say it first and you don't have to say it back if it's not your way. I just wanted you to know how I feel about you these days.'

Ruby stared at him wordlessly, still clutching the pendant he'd given her, the heart currently residing around her neck. She opened her mouth to say those three little words back to him but those words, they simply wouldn't come.

'I've missed you so much,' she said weakly. 'I'm so glad you're back.' Her next words came out in a panicked rush. 'I'm still working on the love thing.'

'It's okay, Ruby. Not everyone jumps off cliffs the way I do. Not everyone wants to.'

'I want to,' she said earnestly. 'I do. I'm standing on the cliff edge and I've just watched you leap off it and my heart is in my mouth for you, and my knees are shaking, and why the *hell* didn't you wait for me, Damon, so we could have done this together? Because now I'll have to jump off that cliff all by myself.'

'No, you won't,' he said with a wry smile. 'I'll jump with you, Ruby. Any time you're ready. First time's always the hardest. Next time might not be too bad at all.'

'Next time *wait for me*,' she commanded fiercely and then drew him to her and wrapped her arms around him and simply held him close and tried to clamp down on her fear of saying those words and meaning them and then not having them be enough. She squeezed him tightly and pressed her lips to his cheek and then the side of his mouth and then she kissed him full on the lips and felt him shudder in return. 'What's it like?' she whispered because she really had to know.

'Oh, you know,' he said raggedly and rested his forehead gently against hers. 'Freefall.'

Life with Ruby in Hong Kong held a fascination for Damon. Ruby got things done with a speed and attention to detail that entranced him. She made his world move with a brightness and lightness he couldn't explain but what it meant was that he could stand utterly still in the middle of it.

And be completely content.

And then Ruby's solicitor phoned through one morning and asked her to drop by the office, and a tremor slid through Damon's shiny magic world. A premonition, if you like, that Damon's sins might be coming back to bite him.

Ruby's feelings for her father were complicated.

Hell, *Damon's* feelings for her father were complicated.

For thirty years Harry Maguire had played the game and kept his secrets in and his daughter out. Thirty years.

Damon didn't know whether to hold him up as a role model or pity him for being so blind.

Damon drove them to the solicitor's offices while Ruby fretted. As soon as they arrived the assistant took one look at them and sent them straight in.

Harry Maguire's solicitor was gimlet-eyed and silver-haired. An old college friend of her father's, so Ruby had said, and there was something in the way the man eyed him and shook his hand as Ruby introduced them that made Damon wonder who exactly this man was and whether he'd known of Harry Maguire's alternate life and whether he knew more than he should about Damon's.

The pleasantries seemed to go on for ever and then the solicitor sat them both down and headed for the other side of the desk and pushed an A4 envelope across the desk towards Ruby.

'This was delivered this morning but before you open it you need to prepare yourself for bad news.'

'How bad?' said Ruby.

'There is a death certificate in there, Ruby,' he said gently. 'I've had it verified. I'm sorry. Your father's dead.'

Ruby barely flinched. Half expecting it, thought Damon. Not sure what to think, feel or do.

'How?' she said threadily, and left the envelope untouched. 'And when?'

'It's hard to say.' The solicitor cleared his throat. 'British Intelligence found his body two days ago. Their report is extremely brief. The coroner's report lists both the time of death and the cause of death as unknown. Harry's body is currently in a London morgue. I can arrange to have it sent on. Anywhere you like.'

'New York,' said Ruby faintly. 'There's a family plot in New York and burial arrangements are in place there. I'll have to phone home. I'm just assuming…'

Ruby put her hand up as if to straighten her headband but she didn't have one on. Her hands went in her lap after that. 'I'm hoping the family will allow him to be buried there. He was blood, even if he was a disgrace to them.' Her chin came up. 'If not I'll make other arrangements. Start a new family plot.'

Loyal to the end. For Ruby there was no other way.

'Your father's assets and accounts have been unfrozen,' said the solicitor, taking back the envelope and unloading it, seeing as Ruby hadn't done so. He found the paperwork he wanted, passed it over to her and this time she took it. 'I have your father's will here, and now that we have a death certificate we can get started on—'

'Did they recover the money?' asked Ruby.

The solicitor frowned. 'British Intelligence makes no mention of it. Anyway, there are no surprises when it comes to your father's will. You're his sole beneficiary. I can start—'

'So they didn't clear him of the theft,' said Damon.

'No, but the release of his assets would suggest—'

'Why don't you ask the British to release Harry Maguire's employee number?' suggested Damon grimly. 'That should clear a few things up.'

'Young man…' The solicitor sat back slowly in his chair and steepled his fingers. '*That* is a very unusual suggestion. One has to ask oneself what could be gained by such a request. May I suggest that the answer would be very little?'

'Oh, I don't know,' drawled Damon. 'What's a daughter's belief in her father's essential goodness worth? What's the knowledge that a man spent thirty years protecting his daughter from the dangers his intelligence work engendered actually worth? What's a man's reputation worth, for that matter?'

'Not a lot,' said the solicitor softly, and rested his head back against his chair, his impenetrable grey gaze fixed on Damon. 'In the grander scheme. Perhaps it's a matter of perspective.'

'Yes,' said Damon agreeably. 'Perhaps it is.'

'Stop,' said Ruby shakily. 'Both of you, *stop!*'

Now the solicitor turned his gaze on Ruby and Damon could have sworn he saw a flicker of grief cross the older man's face. The solicitor sighed, tapped his fingertips together several times, as if coming to a decision.

'Your father was a great asset to us all, Ruby,' said the solicitor, and Damon's eyes narrowed at the other man's choice of words. 'But I fear the restoration of his reputation would prove far too costly for all concerned, including you, and also—if I may be so bold as to dispense a warning—your very intriguing young Mr West. You need to let this go.'

The wily grey fox stood up and went to the door. Opened it to signal the end of their audience with him.

'I'm sorry, Ruby. I've already done everything I can,' he said as she reached the door, her face blank and her eyes stark. 'Your father knew the risks.'

The drive back to the apartment took for ever. Ruby stared out of the window. Damon drove and tried to keep his attention on the road. He shouldn't have said anything. Or saved it for another day. *A never day*, a voice in his head whispered quietly. *You knew this information was going to remake Ruby's world.*

But the way Harry Maguire had been dealt with enraged him and recklessness and fury had taken care of the rest.

So he had cut a path through all the lies and delivered up to Ruby some small semblance of truth and a father she could be proud of. That was what he'd been trying to do. That was what the solicitor who wasn't just a solicitor had been trying to do too.

Deliver up Ruby a father she could be proud of.

Surely they had done the right thing?

Ruby stood straight and silent in the lift on the way to their apartment. She could barely get the key in the lock and flinched when Damon went to do it for her.

'I'll *do* it,' she snapped, so he let her, and strode in after her, already knowing he wasn't going to like what was coming up next.

'Would you like something to drink?' he said as she

dumped her satchel on the kitchen counter. 'Brandy? Scotch? Cup of tea?'

'No,' she said. He could hardly hear her. 'How long have you known?'

'Ruby—'

'How long have you known?' Oh, he could hear her now.

'Known what?' He didn't intend insolence, God help him he did not. Just clarification as to what exactly they were talking about.

'That my father was dead!'

Good. Easy stuff first. 'I found out today. Same time as you,' he said soothingly.

'And how long have you known that he worked for the British Secret Service?'

Now the difficult part.

'Since Sydney.'

'Sydney,' she echoed faintly. 'All that time and you never said a word.'

'I didn't know what to say.'

'How about *Ruby your father was a spy and he's probably dead*?'

'Are you sure you wouldn't like a drink?' he said a touch desperately. 'Pretty sure I'd like one.'

'I trusted you!' Her voice cracked on the word *trusted.* 'And you lied to me. You went after that information and you found it and never said a goddamn word until it suited you to do so! Why now? Why couldn't you have just let it be?'

'Because hacking's what I do,' he raged back. 'It's part of who I am, for better or for worse, and because it annoyed me that they had no intention of restoring your father's reputation to you. What good to you is a corpse and a lifetime of unanswered questions? At least now you know what he did and why he died. He wasn't a thief. He didn't abandon you. He did everything he could to *protect* you. Isn't that worth something?'

'Yes, but can't you understand what I've *lost*?'

'Your father,' he answered doggedly, feeling for all the world as if he were back at school. 'Your view of him. But surely this view is better?'

'A *lifetime* spent not knowing him at all, Damon.'

'That's not true. You did know him, Ruby. Just not that part. Everybody keeps secrets.'

But Ruby just stared at him and shook her head. 'Not like he did. Not like you.'

'But I didn't goddamn *keep* your father's secret,' he roared. 'I told you! Not immediately. Not without a hell of a lot of soul-searching, but I told you, and I knew you'd hang me for it and I *still* told you. Because I thought it would *help* you deal with your father's death. Because I love you. What the hell else do you want from me?'

'I want you to leave.' There was no give in her. Just a blistering fury focused directly at him.

'Ruby—' Damon shook his head. 'No. You're in shock.'

'I want you to leave.' Tears had joined the fury and they lashed at him and stripped him bare.

'Ruby, please.' Surely she would see reason soon, wouldn't she? She could *always* argue both sides of a debate. 'You don't want to do this.'

'No, I think I do. Get out. Getoutgetout*getout*!'

Damon stalked to the room they shared, shoved a

handful of clothes and his notebook in his backpack. Time to go, only this time he didn't want to go.

One more. He'd give it one more try.

Back out to the open-plan area to find Ruby with her elbows on the kitchen counter and both hands in her hair. She looked up as he approached and her eyes were wet and haunted but her mouth was tight and grim.

'Ruby, I'm sorry,' he said. 'For the way this played out and my part in it—I'm sorry.'

'I know,' she replied and nodded and tried to smile through her tears. 'I know you are, but it's not enough. Of all the things I've lost today, what hurts the most is losing my faith in you.'

CHAPTER ELEVEN

IT TOOK Ruby three days to find any sort of equilibrium at all. Three days' worth of misery and sleeplessness, exhaustion and tears. Self-realisation was a painful thing.

Word got out that her father was dead and then came the requests for media interviews—which she refused—and the curiosity of just about everyone she came into contact with—which she couldn't do anything about.

She notified the family, including her mother, made preparations for her father's body to be sent to New York. It had been Ruby's mother who'd argued most strongly for Harry to be buried in the family crypt. The answer had been a vehement no in the beginning and then Ruby's mother had got on the phone to every single one of them and two hours later the answer had been yes.

Maybe her mother had known that her husband had worked for a secret intelligence service all along, but Ruby never asked and her mother didn't say.

People kept a secret for a reason. Chose to share it only when that reason no longer existed or the benefit of exposing the secret outweighed the cost.

Something Damon had been trying to tell her, thought Ruby guiltily. Only she hadn't had the heart to listen.

Hadn't had the brain to sift through the incoming information and separate gold from dross.

You're in shock, he'd said, and she'd known even then that he'd been being generous in his estimation of her.

Irrational.

Mean-spirited.

Scared.

Those were the words he could have used.

Lashing out because life wasn't how she wanted it to be. How old was she? Four?

Where was a sensible, sewing-basket-toting nanny when you needed one?

Ruby had walked and walked some more and the mad had finally worn off. All she had left was sorrow and a growing fear that she couldn't make things right with Damon. That he'd seen her in all her insecure glory and had finally had enough.

It was time to go and find him but he wasn't in Hong Kong. Not staying with Russell, not gettable by mobile. Gone, because she'd screamed at him to leave. There'd been no reasoning with her and Damon had known it.

He could be anywhere.

So who would know? Lena? Worth a try. A phone call.

A difficult one, and Ruby knew it was mad but she found an old polka-dot headband and brushed her hair and put it on, and make-up too, and then surveyed herself in the mirror.

'There's my considerate girl,' she murmured and blinked back sudden tears. 'Now go and apologise.'

'Damon's at the beach house,' said Lena when Ruby asked her. 'What the *hell* did you do?'

'I watched Damon put his heart, his career and then our relationship on the line because he thought it would help me to deal with my father's death,' she said quietly. 'And I called it betrayal.'

Lena said nothing for quite some time and then sighed. 'Damon doesn't know the meaning of the word *self-preservation* when it comes to protecting the people he loves. I did warn you.'

'I know,' said Ruby, and closed her eyes. 'And I get it now.'

'Do you love my brother, Ruby?'

'I do,' she said, altogether terrified that it was too little too late. 'And I need to tell it to him straight.'

'Then I suggest you get on a plane and get yourself over here. There's a front-door key stuck in a crack between the laundry door window frame and the wall,' said Lena. 'And, Ruby? Don't take too long. My brother's hurting. Makes me want to hurt you.'

It only took Ruby a day to get to Byron. She hired a car at the airport, got out the map and tried to remember the way to the beach house and eventually found it, still as beautiful as ever.

She knocked on the door and waited. Rang the door-bell and knocked and waited again.

Nothing.

Eventually she found the key and stepped inside, feeling like a trespasser and a thief, and no gorgeous soft furnishings or open pavilion could take that feeling away from her. And then she saw Damon out on the kiteboard and her heart rate tripled again.

How long would she have before he came in? Time enough to get her props in place?

Sliding the house key in the bowl by the door, Ruby chocked the front door open and started bringing things in.

The sea had always been a favourite playground of Damon's. It swallowed up all the energy a person could throw at it and then sat there, mouth wide open, and dared a man to offer up just that little bit more.

Poppy hated it with a fear she couldn't shake but Damon embraced it. Soar or dive, his body rejoiced and his soul got fed and the bleakness that dogged him these days went away.

But he had to come back in eventually, and when his arms were aching and his legs close to breaking he skidded back in over the sand and brought the parachute down and kitted out and started the walk back up to the house, gear in hand.

The first thing he saw was the headband. It hung off the tap he always used to wash the gear. Misty pink and moss green, a timid gumnut baby peeking out from between the folds, and Damon instantly forgot all about the hosing down of toys. Instead he slid the headband from the tap and, clutching it tightly in his hand, high-tailed it through the garden towards the house. 'Ruby?'

She wasn't in the pool and she wasn't in the pavilion. 'Ruby?'

Damon tossed the headband on the low coffee table that stood in the centre of the pavilion and that was when he noticed the envelope. He backed up. Picked it up. It had his name on it. He didn't open it. Maybe she was in the kitchen.

Nope. Now he opened it.

'I'm sorry,' it said. Only it did it in a hundred different languages, some of them numerical, and filled the entire page.

She wasn't in his bedroom either.

Or any of the other bedrooms or bathrooms and she wasn't in the games room.

He found her in the computer room, with her back to him as she sat at his main console, and every last one of his monitors showing the blue screen of death. She wore a pale pink halter dress, and her black work satchel leaned haphazardly against her chair.

Damon leaned against the doorframe and crossed his arms, mainly to stop them from reaching for her. He cleared his throat.

She didn't turn round, just leaned sideways to read from some sort of textbook that she'd propped open with the edge of his keyboard. She kept her fingers poised over the keys.

'Ruby, what are you doing?'

Ruby straightened slender shoulders but she didn't turn round. She'd put her hair up in some sort of elaborate bun and the clip that held it in place had little pale pink hearts all over it. He had no objection to the hearts but he wanted to see her face.

'I'm hacking your computer,' she said and raised a hand towards the back of her neck to capture a stray strand of hair and give it a twirl.

'Right.'

Damon felt his lips begin to curve.

'How's that working out for you?'

'Not good.' She leaned sideways to study the book again. 'I may need lessons.'

He moved closer until he stood behind her. He breathed her in deep but he still didn't dare touch. Instead, he curled his hands over the back of her chair and peered over her shoulder. 'What is it you want to do?'

'Apologise,' she said. 'And leave a message. A really big one. Full screen. Unerasable.'

'Which would you rather use?' he said. 'Polymorphic or metamorphic code?'

'Can I have both?'

'How long have you got?'

'Hopefully a lifetime,' she said. 'But the message has to go up now. Good thing I brought backup.'

Ruby shut the book with a snap and reached down into her satchel, withdrawing a heart-shaped piece of glossy red contact paper. She leaned back in the chair, her skin brushing against the backs of his fingers and her hair bare millimetres from his chin. She put French-manicured nails to the pointy end, peeled the backing away from the contact and then slapped that big fat red heart up right in the middle of his state-of-the-art computer screen.

'That's cheating,' he said.

'Sue me.'

She pulled a felt-tipped pen out of her satchel next and tugged the lid off with a snap. Damon saw the size of that square-tipped sucker, and wondered if she had any intention whatsoever of staying within the lines. 'Ah, Ruby?'

'What?' She leaned forward and started writing across his heart. Big bold capitals that filled it to the brim.

RUBY LOVES DAMON. (permanently)

'Never mind,' he murmured, and waited, and this time she turned around and the silent entreaty in her eyes cut a path straight to his heart, no code required.

'Damon, I'm sorry,' she said. 'My father's secrecy... His whole secret life felt like a betrayal of my life and the relationship I thought I had with him. I couldn't distinguish between his secrets and yours. All I could see was lies and betrayal. I was too blind to see that everything you'd done you'd done for me. To protect me.'

'I shouldn't have gone after the info on your father,' he offered gruffly. 'I knew you didn't want me to. I did it anyway. If I hadn't, none of this would have happened.'

'And I would never have truly known my father.'

Ruby took a deep breath and her chest rose and fell. She tilted her head, not quite a nod but a tiny twitch of resolve.

'What I did to you, and said to you, and screamed at you, was wrong. I'm so sorry. It won't happen again. I won't let it. Can you forgive me?'

'You had a bad day, Ruby. I can't see there being any others like it. And, yes, if you need my forgiveness you have it.'

'I need it,' she said. 'Almost as much as I need to tell you I love you. Because I do love you, Damon, and if you give me the chance I will spend the rest of my life telling you I love you, and showing you that I do, and jumping off tall cliffs with you.' Ruby's eyes began to shimmer. 'If you still want me to.'

'I want you to,' he said quietly. 'And I promise you this. I will never lie to you, Ruby. I will always love you. And as for secrets—'

She put her fingers to his lips and shushed him. 'Keep your secrets, Damon. I trust you.'

He kissed her fingertips and began again doggedly. 'As for secrets, I promise you—'

'Shh,' she whispered, softer still, and replaced fingertips with teasing lips that brushed his briefly and then drew back just a fraction. 'I don't need your promises either, Damon. I only need you.'

'—that I will always tell you and share with you—'

'Shh.' Ruby punctuated her demand with a lingering kiss. 'I love you.'

'—everything—'

'Shh!' Another kiss and this time the stroke of her tongue.

'—I can!' he finished, and drew his head back, even as he drew her into his arms. 'Are we arguing?'

'What? No! I was just trying to—'

'I'm pretty sure we are,' he murmured silkily. 'Arguing, that is.'

'No, we're not,' she said, eyeing him uncertainly.

'*And* we seem to be at something of an impasse,' he continued, and then he slid his hand up her arm and tugged gently on her halter tie and comprehension finally dawned.

'You're right,' she said with a sultry, knowing smile. 'We're arguing. It's terrible. Dear me, what *shall* I do?'

'I have an idea,' he murmured, and picked her up and whirled her round as she peppered his face with kisses. 'How would you like to win it?'

* * * * *

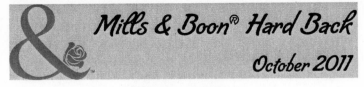

Mills & Boon® Hard Back

October 2011

ROMANCE

The Most Coveted Prize	Penny Jordan
The Costarella Conquest	Emma Darcy
The Night that Changed Everything	Anne McAllister
Craving the Forbidden	India Grey
The Lost Wife	Maggie Cox
Heiress Behind the Headlines	Caitlin Crews
Weight of the Crown	Christina Hollis
Innocent in the Ivory Tower	Lucy Ellis
Flirting With Intent	Kelly Hunter
A Moment on the Lips	Kate Hardy
Her Italian Soldier	Rebecca Winters
The Lonesome Rancher	Patricia Thayer
Nikki and the Lone Wolf	Marion Lennox
Mardie and the City Surgeon	Marion Lennox
Bridesmaid Says, 'I Do!'	Barbara Hannay
The Princess Test	Shirley Jump
Breaking Her No-Dates Rule	Emily Forbes
Waking Up With Dr Off-Limits	Amy Andrews

HISTORICAL

The Lady Forfeits	Carole Mortimer
Valiant Soldier, Beautiful Enemy	Diane Gaston
Winning the War Hero's Heart	Mary Nichols
Hostage Bride	Anne Herries

MEDICAL ROMANCE™

Tempted by Dr Daisy	Caroline Anderson
The Fiancée He Can't Forget	Caroline Anderson
A Cotswold Christmas Bride	Joanna Neil
All She Wants For Christmas	Annie Claydon

Mills & Boon® Large Print

October 2011

ROMANCE

Passion and the Prince	Penny Jordan
For Duty's Sake	Lucy Monroe
Alessandro's Prize	Helen Bianchin
Mr and Mischief	Kate Hewitt
Her Desert Prince	Rebecca Winters
The Boss's Surprise Son	Teresa Carpenter
Ordinary Girl in a Tiara	Jessica Hart
Tempted by Trouble	Liz Fielding

HISTORICAL

Secret Life of a Scandalous Debutante	Bronwyn Scott
One Illicit Night	Sophia James
The Governess and the Sheikh	Marguerite Kaye
Pirate's Daughter, Rebel Wife	June Francis

MEDICAL ROMANCE™

Taming Dr Tempest	Meredith Webber
The Doctor and the Debutante	Anne Fraser
The Honourable Maverick	Alison Roberts
The Unsung Hero	Alison Roberts
St Piran's: The Fireman and Nurse Loveday	Kate Hardy
From Brooding Boss to Adoring Dad	Dianne Drake

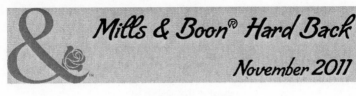

Mills & Boon® Hard Back

November 2011

ROMANCE

The Power of Vasilii	Penny Jordan
The Real Rio D'Aquila	Sandra Marton
A Shameful Consequence	Carol Marinelli
A Dangerous Infatuation	Chantelle Shaw
Kholodov's Last Mistress	Kate Hewitt
His Christmas Acquisition	Cathy Williams
The Argentine's Price	Maisey Yates
Captive but Forbidden	Lynn Raye Harris
On the First Night of Christmas...	Heidi Rice
The Power and the Glory	Kimberly Lang
How a Cowboy Stole Her Heart	Donna Alward
Tall, Dark, Texas Ranger	Patricia Thayer
The Secretary's Secret	Michelle Douglas
Rodeo Daddy	Soraya Lane
The Boy is Back in Town	Nina Harrington
Confessions of a Girl-Next-Door	Jackie Braun
Mistletoe, Midwife...Miracle Baby	Anne Fraser
Dynamite Doc or Christmas Dad?	Marion Lennox

HISTORICAL

The Lady Confesses	Carole Mortimer
The Dangerous Lord Darrington	Sarah Mallory
The Unconventional Maiden	June Francis
Her Battle-Scarred Knight	Meriel Fuller

MEDICAL ROMANCE™

The Child Who Rescued Christmas	Jessica Matthews
Firefighter With A Frozen Heart	Dianne Drake
How to Save a Marriage in a Million	Leonie Knight
Swallowbrook's Winter Bride	Abigail Gordon

Mills & Boon® Large Print
November 2011

ROMANCE

The Marriage Betrayal	Lynne Graham
The Ice Prince	Sandra Marton
Doukakis's Apprentice	Sarah Morgan
Surrender to the Past	Carole Mortimer
Her Outback Commander	Margaret Way
A Kiss to Seal the Deal	Nikki Logan
Baby on the Ranch	Susan Meier
Girl in a Vintage Dress	Nicola Marsh

HISTORICAL

Lady Drusilla's Road to Ruin	Christine Merrill
Glory and the Rake	Deborah Simmons
To Marry a Matchmaker	Michelle Styles
The Mercenary's Bride	Terri Brisbin

MEDICAL ROMANCE™

Her Little Secret	Carol Marinelli
The Doctor's Damsel in Distress	Janice Lynn
The Taming of Dr Alex Draycott	Joanna Neil
The Man Behind the Badge	Sharon Archer
St Piran's: Tiny Miracle Twins	Maggie Kingsley
Maverick in the ER	Jessica Matthews

1011 GEN STD LP